STONE VALLEY SERIES:

A Place in His Heart

The Wilderness Bride

The Lady of North Star

Sandcastles

The Crossing

War Wind

Look for the next exciting novel in the Stone Valley Series!

Novels available for purchase at Amazon.com

STONE VALLEY SERIES:

Book #6

WAR WIND

By

DONNA WHITAKER

Copyright © 2026 by Donna Whitaker. All rights reserved.
ISBN: 979-8-234-04712-0

Model for cover front: Kaylyn Althammer
Photographer: Carla Brock
Cover Design: Griffin Ball

∞∞∞∞∞∞∞∞∞∞∞∞∞∞∞∞

No part of this publication may be reproduced, stored in a retrieval system, or transmitted in any way, by any means, electronic, mechanical, photocopy, recording or otherwise without the prior permission of the author except as provided by USA copyright law.

∞∞∞∞∞∞∞∞∞∞∞∞∞∞∞∞

This novel is a work of fiction. Names, characters, places, and incidents either are the product of the author's imagination or are used fictitiously. Any resemblance to actual persons, living or dead, events, or locales is entirely coincidental.

Dear Reader,

Although Kentucky, during the Civil War, was considered a slave state, and initially tried to stay neutral, the prevailing sentiment of Clinton County, Kentucky citizens was in favor of the Union.

Clinton County was a border county, neighboring Overton and Fentress Counties in Tennessee. Tennessee seceded from the Union in June 1861. The rising tide of secessionism in Overton and Fentress Counties, emboldened the few in Clinton County who favored the South and rebellion.

Clinton County is located south of the Cumberland River. Federal forces stayed primarily north of the river, except for occasional sweeps into Clinton County to drive out the rebels that had crossed the Kentucky/Tennessee line, yet upon their departure, the Confederates always returned. With Union troops occupying the county only occasionally, Confederate soldiers and guerrillas created havoc by stealing and killing in their absence. The time came when a man would not go about alone in the county for fear his horse would be stolen and he could be killed, and in the county seat of Albany only two families remained by the middle of the war.

It was for this reason that Clinton County, Kentucky became known as a county decimated by the Confederates.

A noted and fearsome Confederate guerrilla was Champ Ferguson. The many atrocities he committed in Clinton County, by robbing and outright murder, were grave enough to warrant a trial after the war. Found guilty, he was therefore hung.

My Great, Great Grandfather, Reuben Kennedy lived in Clinton County close to the Kentucky/Tennessee border during the Civil War. He had a large family with four sons enlisting with the Union, two captured and one ultimately dying in Andersonville Prison. Fearing for his remaining family, Reuben changed his name from Kennedy to Canada, moved them to Russell County in 1863, and lived there until his death in 1885.

It is to Reuben and his descendants that I dedicate this book.

CHAPTER ONE

1861

IN EUROPE, the Kingdom of Italy proclaimed Victor Immanuel as king.

In Russia, emancipation of Russian serfs was decreed by the imperial command of Tsar Alexander II.

In America, The Confederate States of America was formed at Montgomery, Alabama on February 4th. Jefferson Davis of Mississippi was elected president and Alexander H. Stephens of Georgia vice president on February 9th.

South Carolina, Mississippi, Florida, Alabama, Georgia, Louisiana, Texas, and other states to follow, seceded from the Union.

Abraham Lincoln was inaugurated as president on March 4th. His first inaugural address stated: "This country, with its institutions, belongs to the people who inhabit it. Whenever they shall have grown weary of the existing government, they can exercise their constitutional right of amending it, or their revolutionary right to dismember or overthrow it." He concluded: "We are not enemies, but friends. We must not be enemies…The mystic chords of memory…will yet swell the chorus of the Union, when again touched, as they surely will be, by the better angels of our nature."

On April 12th the Civil War began at 4:30 A.M. when Confederate shore batteries under command of General P.G.T. Beauregard opened fire on Fort Sumter. The federal garrison, out of supplies, surrendered on April 13th and evacuated the fort the following day.

New Wellington, Kentucky—Stone Valley, Green River Country

Doctor Judah Cross sat in his chair, staring out the window of his library, elbow resting on the arm of the chair, his chin cupped in his hand in contemplation.

It was early morning, the promise of a rainy day appearing, and a hungry coyote trotted across the clearing and disappeared into the woods in search of a meal, but Judah barely gave him a glance.

Interrupting his thoughts, the clock chimed six o'clock. Judah was startled and wheeled his head around to peer at the clock as though he needed confirmation of what he had heard. Restless thinking had plagued him during the night, robbing him of sleep, and, with a deep sigh, he had risen at three o'clock.

Judah rose reluctantly from the chair. He passed by his shelves of books, touching their bound covers reverently with his fingertips, and decided it may be a long time, if ever, that he would seek their knowledge again.

He had read enough about war to know the horrors it could bring. After all, the Revolutionary War was a scant eighty years ago. Before his time, true, but its mark was still fresh enough to him from the reminiscences of a generation past, and Judah was a realist. War was war…period.

Not for him the fervor of the youth of the county. Restless they were, seeking glory for a mission to be accomplished. He was forty-one years of age and, listening to talk of the glory seekers, had become irritated. Why did the young think that dreams were only for them? The old dream also, sometimes with less hope, less anticipation, nevertheless they dream.

His dreams were bound up in home and family, as well as business and church. No…he did not want to go, but had been approached to serve the Union army as a field surgeon, and, after much prayer and soul-searching, finally agreed.

His wife Marnie and their two children, Benjamin and Judith, had departed for Clinton County to be with her father Clay Spencer. In their absence, he had wrapped up affairs at his estate, *The Crossing*, and his hotel, the *Stone Valley Springs Resort.*

Marnie's uncle, Cole Spencer, would manage the hotel as he had for the past twenty years. He had no concerns about that. As the war had started, Judah doubted many patrons would travel to the resort for leisure time anyway.

Leaning against the door frame, his thoughts centered on Marnie, and his mind drifted back to their conversation in this very room about his enlistment.

That Saturday afternoon had been warm and bright, and Marnie had been to New Wellington to shop.

The courier had just left *The Crossing*, and Judah Cross was in the library, seated at his desk and going over the correspondence he was given, when Marnie burst suddenly through the door.

"Was that," she asked, breathlessly and wide-eyed, "who I think it was?"

He glanced up, and, as always, was immediately struck with her beauty, even after twenty years. He was still in awe that it was he that she had chosen to marry when she could have had her pick of many men.

"It was," Judah answered as he shook his head in response.

"Why you, Judah? Why should *you* go?" Marnie cried, despairingly, tears in her eyes. "There are others that could go in your place."

"I know," Judah calmly said.

"After all," she continued, "you have a wife and children."

Judah laid the paper down in silence and poured himself a cup of coffee from the pot on his desk. They had had this conversation several times before, and were always at an impasse. How could he make his wife understand there were times that duty took preeminence over all else?

"I'll do," he said with finality and without meeting her eyes, "what I have to do."

Marnie threw up her hands in frustration. Her mind was working feverishly. Judah couldn't go to war! She might never see him again. She must make him realize somehow that she couldn't do without him.

"Don't you realize, Judah," she protested, "you will be in harm's way most of the time on the battlefield?"

"I'll be in camp hospital most of the time," Judah explained quietly, as he stirred sugar into his coffee.

"Yes," she stated tearfully, "but in harm's way, nonetheless."

"Please, Marnie." He laid the spoon down and his eyes met hers, imploring silence, and comfort. Every line of his face admitted the truth of her words. "Just knowing that you will be waiting for me will give me every reason to live…to come back."

"It isn't tomorrow that I want unless it comes. It's today, Judah!" she declared ardently. "I think about what it means today, if I don't have you!"

He looked at her and tried to find words, and there were none. He glanced briefly at his library of books. Surely, there was some bit of wisdom in them to relay to her the depth of his feelings, but none came to mind. His face was lean with a touch of hardness, with high cheekbones, and a strong jaw. He'd always had a certain loneliness about him, and only Marnie came the nearest to breaking through his reserve at times.

He turned to look at her again. In a sense, they were both alike. She was strong-willed, independent, and somewhat stubborn, traits that attracted her to him, and yet, frustrated him too.

She started to protest again, and then recognized the futility of it. They had had this conversation many times and his mind was set, and whenever Judah Cross determined to do a thing, there was no changing it, for once a course of action was settled on, he did not puzzle about it. She watched him in silence for a few moments, feeling that she would strangle at the pain in her throat.

Her face shadowed with sadness, Marnie turned away, wordless and forlorn, and his eyes dropped away from her retreating back.

He loved her more than anything in the world, had stifled the desire to rise from the desk and take her in his arms, yet this was something he must do. She had accused him of aspiring to fame, but he was no hero. There was a great necessity, and as a doctor, he was merely responding to that need.

Judah walked through his home, caressing every object with his eyes, determined to not forget the splendor that Jake Templeton had willed to him as his inheritance. Merely a poor boy raised on the estate called *The Crossing*, it had come as a surprise to him, as well as others, that he was to inherit everything. He—a boy growing up here, without recognition of a father. He understood it all now, and thanked God that he learned the identity of his real father…an identity that had been kept secret for his own protection. A man he had already loved as a father since infancy. Clell Benson was dead now, but the last twenty years receiving recognition from Clell as his real father, settled him in a way he had never known.

He had done well the last two decades, buying the resort hotel, meeting influential people. But it was such a time as this that brought home the fact that all the work in accomplishing his assets could become just a memory to those he would leave behind.

Judah had listened to the elderly speak in wistful tones of years past and had been taciturn about their musings. Today, he understood their feelings clearly. The wind of caution was wending its way throughout the country as tensions were building. For God and Country was the prevailing thought in some quarters, and States Rights in others.

He was leaving all behind to serve his country as a Union field doctor.

His uniform was laid out on his bed, and with a heavy heart, he turned and slowly climbed the stairs.

Hunching his shoulders against the pelting rain, Judah Cross slipped his hand beneath his cape to assure himself his pistol was still in position. He was on his way to muster in at Camp Dick Robinson at Danville, Kentucky.

Departing through the gate of *The Crossing*, he reined his horse a quarter turn under some trees and, under his slouch hat, stared back at the big house and surrounding buildings. He had spent his whole life here, buried his mother here, married Marnie Spencer, and borne two children here.

"Will I," he muttered softly, "return to see this place again?"

Minutes passed…the rain had tapered to a soft drizzle, and Judah heard the sound of walking horses. Two horses…two riders. Judah pulled his watch from his pocket, opened it, glancing at the time. Right on time, he noted as suddenly he recalled this gold watch had belonged to Jake Templeton…the only thing of value from his estate he was taking with him.

Carefully wiping off the few drops of rain from a branch that had splattered the watch, and with a gentle click, he shut it and returned it to his pocket.

Two riders came into view as they rounded the bend. John "Curly" Matthews and Hardy Harrison. They were mustering in at Camp Dick Robinson also. They were young, but seemed to have a more sensible head on their shoulders than others in the county.

"All set?" Curly asked Judah, without drawing rein.

Judah fell in beside them and pulled his hat a little lower on his forehead. "All set," he answered, and set his eyes straight ahead, all the while thinking of his blonde-haired wife, Marnie.

CHAPTER TWO

Albany, Clinton County, Kentucky
Saturday, July 27, 1861

THE CLINTON COUNTY SEAT of Albany was humming like a beehive. Organized bands of rebels from Overton County, Tennessee, had time and again entered Clinton County to steal horses and plunder. The Southern guerrillas had precipitated the forming of the Clinton County's Home Guard and the subject of war, as well as militia drilling and troops forming, were the chief topics of conversation where any gathering occurred.

To this last, the advocacy of the Union in recruiting men was relentlessly engaged in by two of the town's leading attorneys. If anyone in the town on this day was a Confederate sympathizer, it was not known publicly.

The Stars and Stripes were fluttering in the breeze above the tops of the houses. A procession of thirty-four women on horseback, one of whom carried the National banner, followed by sixty horsemen escorted John Tuttle along with a group of men and a young woman into Albany amidst the shouts of the large crowd assembled there.

Marnie and Judith Cross sat in the buggy in front of Jonathan P. Pickens' Store as the procession passed by.

“Oh, Mother,” cried Judith as she hugged the frame of the buggy, her eyes excitedly scanning the crowd, “Isn’t it wonderful? I’ve never seen anything like it, not even in New Wellington!”

“I suppose so, Judith,” answered Marnie, her own interest rising suddenly.

Marnie’s enthusiasm had nothing to do with the crowd of about two thousand people gathered in town, nor the fact that Colonel Thomas E. Bramlette was giving a speech today on behalf of the recruitment effort for the Union infantry.

She had spotted an old beau, Seth McCord, sitting astride his horse nearby.

“Go find your Grandfather Clay, Judith” Marnie urged, giving Judith a little shove. “I’ll be along directly.”

“All right, Mother,” Judith answered, giving her mother a questioning look, and then descended the buggy. “But don’t be long,” she said, a frown creasing her forehead.

“I won’t,” Marnie answered.

As Judith walked away, and Marnie looked again toward Seth, she remembered, as from a dream those years ago, their youth. So much time spent together, from the time they were children until they were grown. She’d had few girlfriends while growing up in Clinton County and Seth had been her best friend. He was close enough to the buggy, and she saw, as if for the first time, how proudly his head sat upon his neck, how his brown eyes still had that soft look to them. She remembered how kind he had been, the dances and church dinners they had attended together, the many rides on the bridle paths, the crunching of leaves beneath their feet on the trails they walked, and the expectation from the community they would marry.

As though he sensed her eyes upon him, he turned his face from the parade and searched the crowd until his eyes rested on her. As though he could not believe what he saw, he sat still, then: those on foot gave way as Seth McCord carefully edged his horse toward Marnie’s buggy.

He dismounted, and reaching her, took her hands in his.

"Marnie! Surely, it can't be you!" he exclaimed, and his look of utter pleasure nearly took her breath away.

"Seth! Oh, Seth! You recognized me!"

"Recognized you?" said Seth, warmly. "How could I help but recognize you?" He laughed and released her hands. "You haven't changed a bit in twenty years."

"Nonsense!" she protested, but she sounded pleased. "We've all changed."

"If you have, my dear, it's for the better."

Seth searched her face intently. She was more than attractive. She was lovely in a mature way, a way that a man his age could easily settle down with.

And she: she wanted desperately to ask him about his sweetheart for she heard he had one. For a moment her imagination flamed at the thought that he was still single. Then she caught herself with a sniff and reminded herself that she was a married woman...a happily married woman, at that.

"How are you, Seth? It's been a long time."

"So it has," he answered as he settled himself lazily against the buggy.

"How are your children?" he asked.

"How did you know that I have children?"

Giving her a furtive look, "I've kept up with you through Clay," he answered.

"Oh, I see." She thoughtfully looked toward the direction that Judith had gone. "Well, Judith is with me here today, as well as Benjamin." Her eyes grew anxious and she flashed her eyes toward him and nearly grabbed his arm. "Benjamin wants to enlist and serve in the same company with his father," she said. "I have tried to talk him out of it. I've been successful so far—but, oh, Seth! I'm so worried. He's not old enough, you see, and I'm afraid he'll lie about his age with all this talk of war. It has the young men in a frenzy to fight."

“Well,” said Seth as he nodded, “it seems everyone feels the same way. Just look at all the people in town and the way they are carrying on. You would think it was a Fourth of July celebration.”

Marnie’s face was a study. She started to speak, then; faltered. She dared not voice her opinion, for which camp of the war Seth stood loyal to, she did not know. He had given no indication to her that he was joining either side.

“And, Judah,” Seth asked, his face bland, “is he here with you today?”

She hesitated a little and then said: “No. He left for Camp Dick Robinson.”

Seth’s brows lifted at those words and he grew silent. “I’m surprised,” he finally said, softly, “surprised that he would leave *you*.”

Her head lifted abruptly at those words. Seth had hit a sore spot with her. She struggled in her mind daily about that very thing. ”How *could* he leave me?” was the first thought in her mind every morning, and the last when she retired for the night. And now, to hear it audibly from someone else, drove those words afresh in her heart like a stake and she nearly wept.

“They—you see, the Union,” she explained, her voice quavering a mite, “needed his services as a surgeon.”

“Oh, yes, I do see,” he remarked thoughtfully, after a few moments. “Are there no other men in Green River Country they could recruit for such a position?”

Her eyes dropped before his. “He’s one of the best,” she answered with studied coolness. Guilt rose within her breast. She should have sent Judah away with love and prayers instead of resentment, and now it was too late.

Seth watched her with keen interest. “I’m sure he is,” he agreed mildly.

“Are you still practicing medicine, too?” asked Seth.

"Not as a skilled surgeon like Judah, of course," she told him as her eyes darted back to his face, "but I've trained quite a bit with him, and I'm still dispensing herbs."

"And, so…you have come to stay with your father Clay," he stated quietly, shifting himself to better see her face, watching her, reading her with a knowing eye.

Everything within Marnie felt distinctly uncomfortable, and she wanted to squirm under his gaze as color seeped into her cheeks at his scrutiny, but she kept her composure. Did he guess how she was feeling…the regrets she was having?

"How about you, Seth?" questioned Marnie abruptly as she smoothed out an imaginary wrinkle in her dress. "Did you ever think about getting married?"

"No," he said, softly, and looking at her pointedly, his eyes began to gleam oddly, "and you know why."

Her eyes shifted immediately to his. Yes, she did know, that she couldn't deny. She had grown up with Seth and he had wanted to marry her, and she, as well as everyone else thought they would. But Judah had come to live for a while with her father, and she fell in love with him. Seth could not reconcile himself to the fact that she had chosen Judah instead. Even the morning of her wedding he came to her with one last plea. Seth was her friend, a special friend, and, to her, could never anything more than that.

"I've never forgotten you," he persisted, and gave her a slightly sardonic smile. "You know that, don't you?"

She ducked her head and was silent for a few moments. It was a heady feeling to know that Seth had loved her all this time. There was something she had read about unrequited love in a book of poems Judah had, but never experienced such a thing herself.

"That was a long time ago, Seth," she murmured.

"They say," he told her, "that time changes things. I have not found that to be particularly true concerning you, though. Things haven't changed—haven't changed in the least."

She blushed at that, a blush that did not go unnoticed by Seth McCord.

But reality forced Marnie to face the facts. Seth may have yearned after her all these years, but she realized that people often settle for someone else out of loneliness.

Sudden bravado caused Marnie to lift her head in defiance. "I've heard differently, Seth."

Seth McCord leaned forward a little. "Oh?" he asked, his eyebrows rising in interest, the closeness of him unsettling to her.

As she waited for further questions from him, it caught her attention that Seth smelled of leather and some faint cologne that was familiar to her. Marnie refrained from any facial expression as she thought. Oh, yes…she finally realized. It was the same smell of her grandfather Judge Sam Spencer. Odd…that such a thing occurred. If she closed her eyes, she could imagine Grandfather leaning against this very buggy.

"Tell me, then…what have you heard?" Seth asked, at last, drawing her attention back to his state of marital affairs.

"Well—" She hesitated, and, then looking at her hands, gathered courage and blurted, "Well—that you have a sweetheart and that you are going to get married."

He did not answer, and with blushing cheeks, she lifted her eyes to look directly at his. "Are you, Seth?"

She had been so curious about that after Mae, her father's housekeeper, told her, that she could not help but ask him point-blank. She felt a pang of jealously, although just why she should feel that way about him getting married, she did not know.

His eyes were suddenly alert, and he asked, "Would it matter much to you if I did?"

Her blush deepening, Marnie tucked her face down again, and answered in a muffled voice, "Of course, it does. You're my friend."

Seth laughed suddenly, and said, "Look at me, Marnie."

She looked up unwillingly.

"You can tell your sources of gossip that when I get ready to marry, I will announce it myself."

Now she was confused, for his answer was no answer at all. She wanted to pursue her line of questioning for she had been told that his intended was none other than Felicity Morgan, daughter of Jess Morgan, Judah's uncle.

"I—" The expression on Seth's face made her falter. Looking into Seth's eyes, she dared not ask, for his look forbade any further questioning.

"How is your mother?" she asked, instead.

"She passed away last year."

"I'm sorry to hear that."

"Yes…well," he said, positioning himself better against the buggy. "Dreadful time, this is…all this war going on. You heard about last night, didn't you?"

"There was some talk," Marnie admitted. "What exactly happened?"

"Some riders spread the alarm that Confederate guerrillas were coming. About three hundred of the Home Guard gathered in town here and waited for them, but they never showed." He frowned. "I've got a bad feeling about this war."

Seth watched the last of the parade pass. "Look around," he said solemnly. "Everyone cheering, excited about the fight, thinking it will quickly be over, but this war isn't going to be a picnic. They'll find that out soon enough."

Judah had told her the same thing before she left Stone Valley, and to temper her feelings, she tried to toss it off as nonsense. War could not possibly come to Kentucky. Now she was stunned to know that Judah and Seth thought the same way.

"Do you really think," she asked, wide-eyed, "it will be that bad for us? Kentucky is a neutral state, you know."

"Mark my words, Marnie, it won't be neutral for long," answered Seth, his voice a shade grim. "It's a war wind coming to Clinton County."

"War wind?" she questioned, a perplexed look on her face. "But didn't Major-General Buckner enter into neutrality agreements with General McClelland at Cincinnati for the Union and Governor Harris of Tennessee for the Confederacy? I've heard about secessionists in our state, but thought surely we would be safe here in Clinton County."

"We're a border county, Marnie," he explained patiently. "We border Tennessee and that state's voters, last month, chose to secede from the Union. Governor Harris has sent cavalry and infantry into Fentress County right across the line. If he still considers us neutral, his actions contradict his rhetoric. There will be trouble, for sure, for we have Southern sympathizers right here among us in our own county.

"I was building a new home when I read the Louisville newspaper headlining the fall of Fort Sumter," he said. "I knew that meant war and called the carpenters in and told them I was not finishing a house that would probably be burned. They made it livable enough for me to live in though."

"You actually believe," she said, astonished, "that things will go that far? Our homes will be destroyed, right here in Clinton County?"

"Yes, I do. They're already burning the homes of Union supporters in Overton County, Tennessee and it neighbors Fentress County. The Union soldiers will stay north of the Cumberland, I am told, and, therefore, will help us very little. Of course, our speechmakers won't tell us that. It will be nothing for Confederates to cross the county line into our county of Clinton, for Albany is only six miles from the border. Think about it, Marnie. Clay's farm is only three miles from the Tennessee line, so he is in immediate danger. And my place is even closer."

Marnie caught his arm. Her face was pale. "But, Seth—can't the men of this county drive them back across the line?"

“We have Home Guard, yes,” Seth answered soberly, “however, the vast majority of Clinton County’s men will soon be enlisting, and will be gone from this area. There will be too few of us left.”

She sank back in the buggy in horror.

Confederates… in Clinton County! On Pa’s farm!

“Take my advice, Marnie,” Seth told her, “tell Clay to stock up while he can, but store it where the rebels can’t find it.”

Perhaps I was wrong to come back here.

“Maybe I should send my children back to Stone Valley,” she thought out loud. “At least, they should be safe there.”

“I think,” he advised somberly, “you should leave and go back home with them.”

She shook her head. “I can’t. My father needs me. You see, his housekeeper, Mae has been sick this winter. She hasn’t regained her strength and I’m assuming most of her duties.”

“Take him and her with you, then.”

“Pa won’t do that,” she said thoughtfully as her father and daughter approached the buggy. “He’ll never leave that place of his.”

A part of Seth was concerned about her staying in the county, yet…his heart raced a little to know that she would be near him once again. She was married, yes…but he still loved her after all these years, and though it would be bittersweet, to him it would be as though she weren’t. To recapture those memories into the present day would have to be enough.

“Then since you insist on staying,” he said evenly as he straightened and turned to his horse, “should you need me, you know where to find me.”

Seth McCord swung into the saddle, tapped his finger to his hat to her, lifted a hand to Clay Spencer, and rode slowly away.

CHAPTER THREE

SEVERAL HOURS LATER, dinner was over and the crowd in town moved about a half mile outside its perimeter for the speech by Colonel Bramlette. The air was still. Heat waves rippled. The speech ran on for three hours, and Marnie thought several times about leaving, and she would have, too, if it were not for the fact that her father and children were there. And, of course, should she leave, everyone would think her unpatriotic, and it was important to keep her opinions to herself, for she feared the crowd would take her for a Confederate sympathizer.

It seemed every man and woman present at the speech was radiating with an emotion she did not feel. An undercurrent of driving excitement permeated the crowd, but, to her, all the war meant was that her husband was gone, and the county would soon be devoid of most of its men. Why, even some women were talking about following their husbands to help with the cooking and the washing in camp! Had the world gone mad?

How could these women look upon their sweethearts, husbands, and sons with such love, devotion, and worship, and encourage them to enlist? Surely they were listening to Colonel Bramlette as he told of the horrific battle at Bull Run with three thousand casualties in Virginia just a few days ago! And that was just the Union side. Didn't they realize their men may never come back as some of them that fell on the battlefield would not? That thought renewed a dreadfulness in her mind. Judah was gone. Would she ever see him again?

Judah had encouraged her to pray when she felt that way, and she had tried. But the prayers would not form, and there fell on her a dreadful fear she would never see him again. She wanted to cry but the tears would not come. What was that Scripture? "Yea, though I walk through the valley of the shadow of death, I will fear no evil." To her, this war was nothing but the shadow of death, and she was afraid, indeed.

At times the cheering of the crowd was deafening, but she was seeing things they could not…or did not want to see. Who would do the plowing and planting, the weeding and hoeing? Who would take care of the livestock, the fencing, run the cattle, and a hundred other chores to be done?

Marnie felt someone tap her on the arm, and she turned, expecting to see her father. Yet, taken by surprise, it was not him at all. It was Judah's cousin, Duke Morgan smiling at her. It had been twenty years since their last meeting.

"Duke!" she exclaimed, attempting to lift her voice above the din of the crowd.

Duke shook his head, frowning at the crowd, grimly at the unclouded sky, and taking her by the arm, he motioned, with a jerk of his head, for her to go with him. Working their way through the crowd, he led her away to a house with a single sapling tree in the yard.

"What a surprise, Duke, to see you here."

"How so?" he asked.

"I don't know. I guess I just never expected it."

She looked toward the house and yearned to sit on the porch in the shade of the climbing roses and intertwining honeysuckle to rest and escape the heat, but dared not. If caught, they could be misconstrued as intruders, and with the threat of guerrillas in the air, people were on edge anyway.

No…the tree would have to do, and thankful she was, to have it in the blazing sun. At this moment, she felt a little bit like Jonah in the Bible who was thankful for the vine that offered him protection from the sun.

Touching a low branch, she stole a quick look at Duke.

Duke Morgan was a tall man, lean-hipped and broad shouldered with brown hair curling about his neck. A man in his mid-forties, his hair was as brown and without gray as the last time she saw him.

As Marnie stood in the spare shade of the tree, tendrils of blond hair curled against her neck, tiny beads of perspiration on her upper lip, Duke Morgan examined her face a few moments. It had been many years, and though he was attracted to her, she appeared as self-possessed now as before…so annoyingly so, that it had puzzled and disturbed him. It was something he was not accustomed to in women, and it disconcerted him.

"I heard you were back in Clinton County," Duke finally said as he leaned carefully against the trunk of the sapling and crossed his arms.

"And you haven't been to see me?" she softly chided, giving him a smile.

"I thought it best to stay away. I have the feeling," he said evenly, "that your father doesn't think much of me."

"Oh…you think so?" she asked, an innocent look on her face. "If that's the case, maybe he doesn't know you as I do."

He quietly looked at her, then took a cigar from his coat pocket and clipped the end with his teeth. He studied the cigar while he framed an answer and struck a match. Looking past the cigar as he lifted the match, he said, "A lot of time has passed since I saw you." Lighting the cigar, he threw the match away, and grimly said, "People change."

Marnie searched his face as he appeared lost in thought. She had heard he had lost a wife in childbirth, his father was also gone, yet he was a well-to-do man. He was also fortunate enough to remarry and have a daughter survive the birth and grow to her teen years.

Though he was Judah's cousin, Judah made no secret of the fact that he, as her father Clay, believed that Duke had a mean streak in him. She felt Judah's opinion of Duke was due to jealously, for Duke was a beau of sorts, so to speak, at one time.

A sudden smile lit his face, his brown eyes dancing in merriment, and Marnie recognized the old charm again. There *was* something stimulating about him, something warm and electric. He was known in the past to have a reputation with women, and she had determined long ago not to be a statistic in his tally book, although she, full of mischief, flirted with him whenever the occasion presented itself.

"Enough about that," he said, turning his full attention on her. "Tell me, my dear Marnie, just how long will you be here?"

"I'm not sure," she said, smiling in return. "Judah has enlisted and is at Camp Dick Robinson. I—I just don't know." Her face turned serious. "This war business is unsettling everything."

"What do you mean?"

"Well, for one thing, Judah has left. I tried talking him out of going, but he wouldn't listen to me. All I hear is from everyone is war talk."

Duke looked toward the crowd and the smile left his face and, in its place cynicism and contempt.

"Impetuous lot, aren't they?" he derided.

Marnie looked at him and wondered how it was possible to convey such disdain in that look. "Impetuous?"

"You know—rash, hotheaded, unthinking. Their kind fight the wars of this world and get nothing but a lonely grave somewhere. They're rushing to battle—oh, I know," he said at the look on her face, "the leaders of this county think this is a glorious cause, to fight for the Union. However, I just want to be a spectator and do not want to be involved, and I'll wager you don't either. I watched your face in that crowd. You have an easy face to read, you know. You didn't want to be there in the sweltering sun, listening to speeches, hearing cheers in response, any more than I did."

"Wha—?" Marnie said, taken aback.

As Duke continued, fear gripped Marnie. As careful as she was, she didn't think her feelings showed. What would people think of her? She would have to take greater care from now on. She didn't have to talk in favor of the war; then again, neither did she have to talk against it.

"Well, one thing is for sure," Duke said, "we'll see what the Old Man has to say about this whole thing."

"The Old Man?" Marnie asked, puzzled.

He smiled. "You know." He pointed his finger upward. "As we say, God in heaven."

She had never heard God described as the "Old Man" before. Certainly not among her acquaintance and she thought his religious notions rather queer.

"I'm just…a little tired right now, Duke," she said, wiping the back of her hand across her forehead. "Perhaps you read me wrong."

Duke searched her face again and drew on his cigar in thought. "I think not, Marnie," he finally told her.

"Why—" Marnie began, and then hastily checked herself. She wasn't against war itself, as he apparently thought, if it did not affect her personally, but she was a practical person, recognizing that war was not all glory, but danger and suffering. Those very things made her look beyond today's emotional affectations in anticipation of tomorrow's pain. The thought that Duke considered her unpatriotic, and heartily approved, stiffened her spine.

"But, Duke," she protested, "where would we be today if our ancestors had not fought in the Revolutionary War? Still under England's rule, that's where we'd be. There *are* times, whether we like it or not, that we must fight for what is right and—"

"Forget it," Duke broke in, hands held high, palms out. "Forget it. I'm not looking for a fight with you. Leave the fighting to others. After all," he smoothed her with a quick smile, "we *are* old friends, aren't we?"

He looked around and, with surprise, noticed the crowd was disbursing and evening was drawing near.

"It seems we are about to have company," he motioned toward Clay Spencer and Judith approaching with a disapproving look on her face, and with his usual charm, Duke introduced himself to Judith as an old friend of the family.

"Duke Morgan?" Then: recognition at the name lit Judith's face. "You're my father's cousin, aren't you?"

"Second," he said, taking off his hat. "Second cousin. Yes, I am, miss."

Clay Spencer's eyes measured Duke Morgan, searching, but asking no question.

"Isn't it all exciting, Mr. Morgan," Judith chirped, "the speeches and enlistment of our men?"

Duke shrugged his shoulders. "You know there's a saying, 'If you live by the sword—'"

"Yes, well..." Clay interrupted and, leaning toward him, said, "At times, such as this, there is a cause...a *good* cause."

Duke had not joined the Home Guard as some other men in the county had, and Clay thought perhaps there might be lurking the heart of a Confederate sympathizer within him. "Just what side are you on, Duke?" he asked bluntly.

"I?" Duke answered, eyebrows raised. No one had asked his opinion on the matter before and he wondered if he should sidestep the issue. But true to form, Duke finally replied, "I take no side," and put the cigar in his teeth.

"No?" Clay commented dryly. "Before this is over, I venture you *will* choose," he challenged.

Duke's face went white. He took the cigar from his mouth and looked at the end of it. He then threw his cigar away, looking disbelieving at Clay. His eyes twinkled a little and only his eyes were smiling...not the smile of amusement, but of disdain.

"We shall see, Clay," Duke said, at last. "We shall see." And with that, lifted his hat to the ladies and sauntered away.

"Pa! Was that really necessary?" scolded Marnie when Duke was out of earshot. "He's an old friend."

“Be careful of him, Marnie,” Clay warned as he watched Duke disappear into the crowd. “You don’t know him like I do. There’s some talk that it was he who killed a constable in Tennessee not long ago and he’s out on bail. Nobody has proven anything yet, but I’m telling you, Duke Morgan has a side to him you haven’t seen...and this war will bring it out of him.”

Marnie looked at her father curiously. “What did the War between the States have anything to do with Duke Morgan?” she thought. “He’s just a farmer from Clinton County, Kentucky. Is it merely supposition? What does Pa see in Duke that I cannot?”

CHAPTER FOUR

DAWN BROKE BRIGHT and the morning sun lay warm upon the quiet hills. After breakfast, the cattle were started toward the north valley, and the smell of sun-warmed grass was in the air.

It was very early, and Marnie had just cleared the table, and Judith had started washing dishes when Benjamin walked in.

"Why, Ben!" declared Marnie. "I thought about waking you. Any reason why you were sleeping in? Let me get you some breakfast. We have church today. It seems it might be the last service for quite a while with the pastor joining the infantry. What has this county come to? Pastors leaving their churches, and schoolteachers joining up, too. No church, schools closing down. Fair game for anyone needing religion and education now!"

Ben didn't answer, and instead seated himself at the table and watched his mother prepare his plate. Judith rattled on to Ben about meeting Duke Morgan.

"Now, Judith," said Marnie reproachfully, "you know your Grandfather Clay doesn't approve of him."

"I know, Mother. But, honestly, I thought he was a perfect gentleman. I don't understand why Grandfather is so set against him," she argued.

Marnie set the plate in front of Ben, and noticed something was not quite right. "What's wrong, Ben?"

He hesitated while she reached for silverware, and winced when she placed the silverware down a little too hard.

Marnie grasped the back of a chair, fastening her eyes on his grieved face. “What is it, Ben?”

Something was wrong. Something she couldn’t quite put her finger on and she grew anxious. Did it have anything to do with the war? He had disappeared and didn’t ride home with them last night, but came in rather late.

“I—” Ben started.

“Ben?”

Judith stilled her hands on the dish she was wiping, and turned to look at him.

Marnie looked down at Ben, her eyes stared, and with an intentness that made him uneasy.

“Well, Mother.” He paused, and then lowered his head.

“Yes? What’s on your mind?”

Ben put his hands at his sides and dared not look at her face. “All right, Mother,” he blurted out, “it’s like this. We formed a cavalry company under Captain Brents. We’re now officially known as Company C, First Kentucky Cavalry.”

At that answer, Marnie’s face blanched, and lips tightened, and she was filled with a feminine desire for tears. We! We! She grasped the chair harder. What she had feared all along had finally happened. Her son had enlisted!

“Please don’t be angry, Mother,” pleaded Ben, staring at her white face.

For a few moments, while Ben waited with abated breath, she could not speak.

“Enlisted!” she hoarsely uttered. “Is that what you did?”

Ben shifted his eyes from her, and when he did not answer: “Enlisted!” Marnie repeated, ready to swoop down on him. “How—how could you do that? You know I didn’t want you to join! I talked about it many times with you!”

"I know," he said quietly, staring at his plate of food, "but this is something I have to do. Besides, I want to be with Father. He may need me."

"He may need *you*!" She gave an ugly laugh. "Don't you realize that you might get injured and will need *him* as a surgeon?" she argued.

"I was hoping to serve with him as an orderly."

"Ben…" Marnie remonstrated, "you're too young. You have to be twenty-one to enlist, and you must have permission…and *that* I will not give."

"I *do* have permission, Mother," he quietly insisted, looking at her with imploring eyes.

Her eyes opened wide. "What do you mean you have permission? From whom, may I ask?"

"Father gave me written permission before he left."

Marnie was stunned into temporary silence. "Judah gave Ben permission without my knowledge?" she thought. "Not only did Judah leave me, but he is taking my son away, too?"

"I'm nineteen, Mother," he pleaded in her silence as he swiped a hand in the air. "There are others that have enlisted that are younger."

"That may be," she finally murmured through lips that felt too numb to speak, still dazed by the news, "but nineteen is still too young."

In reply to her statement, he argued defensively, shifting in his chair, "It's not too young. I'm a grown man, Mother…it's time you realized that."

Something snapped within Marnie and her face contorted into an ugly expression. "So…you want to be a hero, is that it? Do you know what happens to heroes, Ben? They die, that's what! Maybe you think this war is a struggle for a better way, but I don't see it that way. It's only a destruction of families."

He had heard the same quarrels between his father and mother, and knew the terms on which they had parted. Would she do the same to him as to his father? Would unspoken words of bitterness lie heavily in the air when he left?

"I'm going to Camp Dick Robinson, Mother," he said decisively, and stood up suddenly, shoving back his chair, and it seemed his jaws were a shade whiter. "I must be there in a few days."

Marnie started to make an abrupt reply, but Ben turned and walked briskly from the room, and she heard the front door slam.

Marnie sat down suddenly in the chair and put her head in her hands. Just like his father, he was. Same looks, same personality, same insane reason to leave…neither wanted to listen to her.

"Mother?" asked Judith, apprehension in her voice. "Are you going to let Ben go out without any breakfast?"

After a bit, Marnie raised her head, and said quietly, "No, Judith." With a half-smile, she asked, "Would you be good enough to wrap up some breakfast and take it to him?"

Marnie did as Seth McCord suggested yesterday. He said if she needed him, then to come to him. Well, today is one of those days, she decided. With haste, she saddled her horse and rode to his place this very morning, early as it was, before he had a chance to leave for church.

As for her, listening to the preacher's sermon, encouraging men to enlist, was the last thing she wanted to do right now.

Riding the gradual slope toward the house, she then drew rein when she spotted a man in the yard, standing with a rifle in the hollow of his arm.

Seeing a woman rider, he turned on his heel and called to the house. Then he walked toward the barn. Hesitating, Marnie rode cautiously the rest of the way in, her attention drawn to the new home Seth had been building. The exterior looked nearly finished, and she longed to go inside to see just how much was put in order, but before she could do that, Seth McCord stepped onto the porch.

“Marnie! What a surprise!” he said, as she dismounted and tied the reins. Meeting her on the top step, he took her arm and led her into the house.

“Would you like some coffee?” he asked, stopping inside the door, looking down into her troubled face.

She nodded and when he turned, she followed him to the kitchen.

It had been a long time since she had been here. It was a very small house. Nothing had changed in twenty years except, for the fact, that the front room was littered with clothing hastily thrown over furniture.

When she entered the kitchen, she stood, looking around as though she had not seen it before.

The room was small, only a little light came in the small window, but she noticed the floor looked scuffed and dusty like it hadn’t been swept in a while. There was a sheet-iron stove and a pile of wood near it. Dishes were unwashed, and coats were hung on pegs on the wall and a kerosene lamp stood on the table.

Seth pulled a chair out for her, and, setting a cup on the table for her, poured from a blackened coffeepot.

His mother had always kept the kitchen spotless, and Marnie thought to herself that he truly needed a wife, and said so without taking forethought.

Seth smiled at the implication and asked, “Are you applying for the position?”

Marnie blushed and cast her eyes down as she peeled off her gloves. “I—I—now, Seth,” she softly scolded.

He laughed and returned the pot to the stove. “Just testing the waters,” he quipped, and then sat down at the table.

“That ship,” she answered quietly, “sailed a long time ago.”

“Maybe,” he said, amused, hope ringing in his voice.

“What brings you over this way?” he asked. “I thought there was church today. Someone sick?”

“No…nothing like that. There *is* church today…or should I say the last service.” She faltered, “I—I came to see *you*.”

“I suppose I should feel flattered,” he commented as he pushed the sugar toward her. “Tell me, just why did you want to see me?”

She shook her head no to the sugar. “I needed someone to talk to. I can’t talk to Pa, and it upsets Judith if I talk to her.”

When she hesitated, “What’s the problem, honey?” he asked, tenderly. “You know you can tell me anything.”

His sympathetic tone was nearly her undoing.

“It—it’s Ben,” she said, dropping her head into her hand, trying to keep her voice from cracking. “Oh, Seth.” Her voice was almost pleading in its sorrow. He enlisted last night, in spite of all my warnings about staying out of this war!”

Seth looked at her a few moments, and then shrugged his shoulders. “Doesn’t surprise me any. I saw him hanging around late last night, but I left before he did.”

“And to beat it all, Pa is so head up over the Union,” she continued, flustered. “When Ben told him this morning, Pa was downright excited! He went on and on about the ‘Glory of the Union’ and was telling Ben how proud he was that Ben is taking up arms!”

“Well…yes, most in this county have that attitude right now, it seems.”

“Not me!” she cried out. “I’ve lost a husband to the Union, and now I’ve lost a son.”

“I understand how you feel,” he said guardedly, “but don’t you think you’re overreacting just a bit? After all, they *are* still alive.”

She glared at him, but before she could reply, he said, “Now…smooth your ruffled feathers. I’m just saying, it could be getting Ben out of here may be the best thing for him right now.”

“Why,” taken aback, she exclaimed, “in the world would you say something like that when you know good and well that he’ll be in harm’s way?”

“Marnie, dear, I told you that trouble is coming to Clinton County. You wouldn’t take my advice and consider going back home where you and the children would be safer. Not that there won't be trouble there, mind you, but I'm telling you again, Marnie, it's war coming to this county, more so, I believe, than in some other parts of the state. But you just can't seem to understand that."

Seth stared at her accusingly and, for a moment there, they locked eyes.

"Just what," she suggested, puzzled by his look, "are you insinuating, Seth McCord?"

Seth studied the back of his hands in thought as he pursed his lips. "I saw you with Duke Morgan yesterday evening."

Her temper flared, but she quickly lost her anger and smiled a little. Picking up her cup, she looked over the rim, and asked, softly, "Do I detect a little jealously, Seth?"

He looked sharply at her. "Take care, Marnie," he warned, and her smile faded.

Seth's face was inscrutable, and until he spoke again, she was at a loss to what he meant.

"This is no game, Marnie," he finally said, none too gently.

"Why—I don't know what you're talking about, Seth," she said, slowing putting her cup down.

"This war business, that's what I mean."

"I know we're at war, Seth," she stated emphatically. "Believe me, oh, how I know we're at war!"

He looked at her pointedly for a moment. "You don't understand what I'm saying," he told her.

"All right," she said, becoming frustrated, and shifted in her chair. "Tell me. I'm listening."

"I'm talking about Duke Morgan, for one thing."

"Whatever do you mean?" she asked, mystified. "What about Duke?"

"He could spell trouble for you."

"Why—why, Seth!" she cried, scandalized. "I thought you and Duke were long time friends."

He nodded. "We are—we are…of sorts. I know just how far I can push him," he added, "and when to back off."

How could Duke cause me any trouble? Marnie thought. *We've always got along in the past. Why should now be any different?*

"He's never done me any harm," she said as formally as she could, "if that's what you are suggesting."

"No," he returned to her, "I didn't think that or I would have heard about it. Duke is not known for keeping secrets. I knew he was sweet on you in the past, and that may be to your advantage…and Clay's," he added as an afterthought.

"I don't understand," she said, a little confused, "what you're saying, Seth."

Seth touched his tongue to his lips. "With Judah out of the way," he thought, "Duke might set his sights on Marnie…and that could be either good or bad. And just how would Marnie respond? She was unpredictable, to say the least, and the years had not seemed to change that trait in her."

"Let's just say," he patiently explained, "that his feelings for you may overlook any trouble he might otherwise cause. Of course, he might swing the other way. Since Ben and Judah will be fighting for the Union, Duke may very well stand firm on his political notions in spite of the direction of his heart."

Marnie looked incredulous. "Are you saying, Seth, that Duke Morgan is for the Confederacy?"

"He's never formally declared his political leanings, but there's a strong possibility," he said with conviction.

"But Duke never indicated that he was for the Confederacy when I talked to him yesterday."

"Maybe not," Seth answered, "but he did own slaves at one time. He had to sell them a few years back when he had to get a bond to cover some trouble he was in."

"I didn't know that," she said, thoughtfully.

"No, of course, you wouldn't."

She couldn't imagine the Duke Morgan she knew would turn upon her and her family. But between what her father had said, and now Seth, she began to rethink the matter and started to see Duke

Morgan in a different light…or, at least, a lurking possibility of such a thing happening.

"So," she said, drawing circles with her finger on the table in thought, "you're saying Duke might cause trouble for both Pa and me?"

"He might," Seth acquiesced. "He just might."

"And you," she asked, "is that why you have a man guarding this place? Are you afraid he'll cause trouble for you?"

"No," he answered. "I don't foresee any immediate conflict with Duke Morgan. The fact is, I live too close to the border, and a man can never tell when Confederate guerrillas or troops will cross the county line and try to relieve me of my stock. They will especially be looking for horses and I've got to find a place to hide them. There are caves all over this county. I just need to find a suitable one…a place they would never think to look nor find."

Marnie's mouth turned grim as she digested in silence what he had just told her. Could it possibly get that bad in Clinton County, and especially here close to the border? Would Pa truly lose his livestock? Those horses he has taken great pride in all these years? And the cattle and hogs? What about the crops? What would they do? How would they survive?

A long ago memory resurfaced in her mind and with it a glimmer of hope. She had not thought of it in years. Would her father agree to it?

"Seth!" she cried suddenly, straightening in her chair. "I know the perfect place! Pa found it about twenty years ago when a lot of our stock went missing. Remember? You were a part of the Clinton County Stock Company, too, same as Pa."

"And?" he urged her to go on, curiosity alight in his eyes.

"Well…it was years ago, like I said. I overheard Pa and his hands talking without ever knowing that I did. The way I remember it, Pa tracked the rustlers to a cave. The cave was long and led to a very large valley. That's when they caught Lyle McKendrick rustling and he was killed. Didn't Pa tell you about the cave?"

"No, he didn't," he said thoughtfully. "I knew rustling was going on. They rustled a few of mine, as a matter of fact. And I knew Lyle McKendrick was caught and shot, but Clay never told me about a cave and valley."

"Hmm. Well…I guess Pa wanted to keep the cave a secret for whatever reason. He probably didn't want any other rustlers getting the same idea and driving them there if they knew about it."

She reached over and placed her hand on his. "If you want me to, Seth, I'll ask Pa if you can take your stock there for safekeeping."

"I appreciate that, Marnie," he said, rubbing his other hand across his jaw in thought, "but I think I'll ride back with you and ask Clay myself. I'd like to see this valley you're talking about."

"I'll go with you," she said excitedly, scooting back her chair, reaching for her riding gloves. "I've never seen the valley either, and it just might be that you can talk Pa into driving his stock there, too. To hear him tell it, this war will be over before you know it, and I know he's making no such plans as you're talking about."

CHAPTER FIVE

RIDING ONTO Clay Spencer's place, and approaching the house, Marnie made the comment to Seth that his new home looked a lot like her father's.

Seth laughed as they dismounted and tied the horses to the rail. "You're exactly right. Clay's ranch home was the pattern for my own. I wanted nothing but the best. No two-story home for me."

Marnie thought of her large two-story estate on *The Crossing* in Stone Valley, and opened her mouth to describe it to Seth, but immediately dismissed the idea. Anyway, Stone Valley seemed so very far away just now.

They noisily entered the front door, which brought Mae to the front room. "Your father is having his lunch in the kitchen," she stated as she jerked her head in that direction and headed back that way.

"Thanks, Mae," Marnie said to her retreating back.

Seth was laughing at some comment Marnie made as they entered the kitchen. A smile crossed Clay's face when he saw Seth. He'd always had a great liking for Seth, more so than Judah, for Clay had often thought Judah a man hard to get to know.

Seth was a different matter though. Easy going, amiable, Seth McCord made friends easily, and Clay had wished at times that Marnie had chosen him to wed instead of Judah. At least, he could have had his daughter near him all these years instead of being taken to Green River Country by Judah, a situation which afforded him only a rare occasion of being with her and the children. And, even at that, he had to leave the ranch to be with her.

"Sit and have some lunch," Clay offered Seth, and nodded to Mae to serve.

Seth sat, leaning his forearms on the table; then accepted a plate from Mae with a "Thanks."

Clay looked from Seth to Marnie and back again, then continued eating. To him, they seemed mighty close-knit. "Wonder what Judah would think about that?" he thought.

"What brings you this way, Seth?" he asked, then shoved another forkful of food in his mouth.

"Well, I've been doing some thinking, Clay."

"Um?" Clay asked, concentrating on the plate before him. "What about?"

"You know that last year was a bad year for crops, and have left us short. Not much wheat to speak of, and corn didn't do well. But by the looks of things, it seems we're going to have a pretty good crop this year, though…if we can harvest in time, that is."

Fork in mid-air, Clay looked at Seth, puzzlement on his face. "What do you mean, Seth? Harvest in time? What are you talking about?"

"Clay…you know that many of our men will be leaving to fight for the Union. We've already lost our blacksmith to Company C."

Clay nodded. "So? What's your point? What does that have to do with the harvest?"

"We've got to be thinking and planning what's going to happen when they do leave."

Clay laid his fork down and picked up his coffee cup in thought, trying to anticipate just where Seth might be headed.

"Explain yourself, Seth," he said, after a sip of coffee.

"Listen, Clay," began Seth as he shifted in his chair. "There are Confederate troops gathering at the border. Talk is, the Union troops will stay north of the Cumberland, and that will leave us at the mercy of the States Righters.

"We've got to plan for when they cross the county line and overrun this place. We'll have a few Home Guard folks left, but not nearly enough of what we need. Those Confederate boys will confiscate everything they can lay hands on...crops, horses, cattle...everything. Since I'm close enough to the county line to spit, someone has already stolen a couple of my horses. I don't want to cast disparaging claims about who took them, but I've got my suspicions.

"We've got to find a place where you and I will be able to hide our stock and store what we can harvest. Marnie was telling me about a cave and valley you found twenty years ago. I think you should run your stock in there, and if it's big enough, I'd be grateful if I can drive mine in there also."

Clay set his cup down, pushed back his plate, and drummed his fingertips on the table in thought. He had not thought much about the county being left in dire straits after the boys left to fight. He took for granted the fact that the Union troops would help out.

He had built this place with hard sweat and his own two hands...had some of the best horses in the county. His mind replayed the scenario Seth described. And another thing: was the valley large enough to hold all their stock? It had been about twenty years since he had been there, and he wasn't sure he remembered the way.

"You really think it's going to come down to that?" he finally asked.

Seth wiped his mouth with his napkin and sat back in his chair. "Yes, I do, Clay," he said decidedly. "I surely do."

So caught up in the politics of the war, Clay had not stopped to think what the Secessionists could do to Clinton County. He envisioned their troops invading the land, taking his prized horses and cattle, and anger began to build. No! They would not! If he had to use every bit of strategy to circumvent their actions, he would!

He would move every living thing off his ranch…chickens, hogs, and all!

"Well, whether you're right or not," Clay conceded, at last, "I guess it wouldn't hurt to do as you suggested. Finish your lunch and I'll take you to my valley. One thing is certain, though, this can't get out to anyone else. People talk, no matter how good they are, and especially when they are under pressure."

If there was one thing Clay liked about Seth, it was his farsightedness. And for yet another time, he wished Marnie had chosen him instead of Judah.

Riding past the north pasture, they traveled for an hour, picking their way over hills through a long forgotten trail only frequented now by wildlife. Before long, Clay heard the bubbling of a tumbling stream and turned off the trail, riding towards its sound. Reaching it and continuing for a bit longer, Clay drew rein. "It's shallow here," Clay said, "and will be easy to cross. Come on," he urged, starting his horse across.

Following Clay, they splashed through the water, the click of horses' hooves on stone as they crossed the wide bed of rocks that covered part of the stream bed, and climbed the gentle slope to the other side.

"It's been a long time since I've been here," Clay said, his brow drawing into a frown, "but I think I can find it." His face lit, remembering the way. "Yes, I'm sure this is it. Follow me."

They turned at right angles, and finally dipped into a draw. Riding for another half-hour, they came to a grove of trees with thick underbrush, a wide stream running along the front.

They turned their horses left into the stream and the ground rose up slightly as a large hill projected from the ground. To Seth and Marnie, something seemed wrong with what they were seeing. The hilly ground seemed to be an optical illusion.

Following Clay, they dismounted their horses and led them to what appeared to be a large indentation in the rock. Reaching the rock, there was an opening that ran back into the rock parallel to the face.

"Pa?" Marnie asked. "Are you sure about this?"

"Just picket the horses and follow me," Clay told her.

They secured the horses, and then entered the opening that was no more than six or seven feet in length that seemed to end in a blank wall. When they stepped inside, they felt cool air coming from the left. Just inside the entrance was a shelf head-high on the right. Clay Spencer put his hand up and found a few candles. Clay and Seth each took one, lit them, and then proceeded through the cave which had a high ceiling and was about two hundred feet long.

Seeing light at the end of the cave, they extinguished the candles, and approaching the opening, stood, adjusting their eyes to the light of the sun.

What Clay had remembered as a small valley was not so small, indeed. Large it was, bounded by hills, and with a stream running one edge of the valley. An old lean-to, built by rustlers years ago, was still standing.

"Clay!" Seth exclaimed. "This is a perfect place! Good grass and water. We could hold the stock here for a long time."

Clay studied the lean-to for a minute. They could build a more substantial building, in the event they had to escape here for their lives. If they wiped out the trail their stock would make, no one would be more the wiser that they were here. If the war didn't last very long, this valley would be big enough, indeed. But—what if?

Clay shook his head, clearing his mind of too many suppositions. First things, first. Concentrate on the valley and make it ready. One day at a time had always been his motto, and so it was now.

"All right, Seth," hands on his hips in readiness, Clay agreed. "Time to start is now. Why don't you drive your stock in first, and I'll do something about living quarters. It won't be anything fancy, but this is wartime, and we'll have to make do."

He looked at Marnie. “You might as well forget, for the present, about that fancy house of yours up north,” he said. “I don’t want to hear any complaining, do you hear?”

She smiled at him. “I’m your daughter, aren’t I, Pa?” she said glibly. “What you can take, I can take.”

Clay didn’t smile back and looked at her with consternation for he was worried about her. She was his only child, and was sometimes too sure of herself. She had changed some since Judah was gone, but still….

She was the love of his life. Her mother dying while she was young, he had always let her have her head about things while growing up. He had not considered how she would fare during the war, and now that Seth had opened a window into a future that he had not considered, he was tempted to send her back to Stone Valley. “Hard-headed as she is,” he thought, “she probably won’t go.”

“We’ll see,” was all he said, and he said it with a frisson of unease.

CHAPTER SIX

Saturday, August 3, 1861

"THERE WOULD never again be a day like this one!" thought Marnie as she watched prancing horses, restless, as their riders standing beside them were.

The boardwalks were crowded and the streets lined with wagons, buggies, and saddle horses. Voices were everywhere, and the sound of men's boots and women's slippers was heard on the walks as doors slammed on business establishments.

A week after Colonel Bramlette had arrived in the county a full company of cavalry was ready to leave Albany. They were told to wait until after the elections to depart, but Company C would not be deterred. Depart they would, for their country needed them, and the entire county was assembled to bid farewell to the first company from that section.

Eighty-five citizens had enlisted for three years and among them was Benjamin Cross.

Boys in the Home Guard were there, promising themselves as soon as they were old enough, they would also enlist, if the war lasted that long. Middle-aged men and older men who were left would protect the county from unwanted invaders should they dare cross the county line.

A look of pride was on the faces of all the women, tears of pride on their cheeks, love in their eyes as they turned toward the enlistees. It was high pride and devotion in their hearts. These men were sweethearts, husbands, sons, and neighbors. After all, these men were going to save the Union!

It was a grand gathering, and amid the dogs barking, hurrahs, and endless chattering, Marnie returned to the buggy for a going away gift for Ben. It was a small "housewife" made of flannel with needles and thread, and a pair of small scissors. He would surely find use for it wherever he was going to from Camp Dick Robinson. She clutched the "housewife" in her hand and turned to walk back to the crowd, and found Duke Morgan had sought her out and was approaching her.

"Marnie," he addressed her, with a tip of his hat.

"Hello, Duke," she said, sweeping her blonde hair back where it had fallen over her face. "Goodness, but it's hot! It's a fine turnout today though, isn't it? I suppose everyone in the county is here."

"So it seems."

He looked at her, a certain light in his eyes, as she fanned herself with her hand.

"You know, you're mighty pretty, all flustered like that," he said, with a slow, ingratiating smile.

Taken aback, she turned to him, eyes wide. Men didn't look or talk to a married woman like that. And only those, who were sure enough of themselves, would utter such a thing to a single girl.

Seth's words came back to her. When it came down to it, what would Duke do? Would he be for her or against her? And there was that deal about him killing somebody by—what was that name Pa said? Oh, yes—some constable in Tennessee. *Did* Duke do such a despicable thing? *Could* he? She truly wanted to know.

But she kept her questions to herself and merely answered, "Well, thank you, Duke."

"You know, if you weren't married," he pursued his line of thinking, "I'd fall in love with you all over again."

Marnie laughed nervously. "Well, too bad for you, I *am* married, Duke. And so are you."

He laughed at her apparent unease. "I was in love with you once. Remember?"

"Duke, I don't know that I remember that," she said, dubiously.

"Marnie, you forget easily," he said, with a touch of bitterness. "But I suppose there was no reason for you to remember *me*. It was natural for me to miss you. But you treated me like I was a brother…most of the time, anyway," he added, a hint of teasing in his smile.

"Of course, I was never any competition for Seth McCord. He had you all sewed up…until Judah Cross came along, that is." He looked at her keenly. "But now it seems you've got pretty thick with him again."

"Duke!" she cried, scandalized. "Seth is a friend that I've known my whole life. He and my father are good friends. Have always been, come to think about it. They've been members of the Clinton County Stock Association and done business together. I'm merely there when he comes to see Pa," she argued. "I can't stop the wanderings of your mind, but you're sure taking a lot upon yourself," she said, coldly.

Duke immediately caught her hand, and she was tempted to resist his overture.

"Marnie, I didn't mean to offend you," he hastily proffered. "Like you said, I guess it's just the wanderings of my mind."

Slightly mollified, she said, "No offense taken, Duke. But let's not have any more talk about such things, if you don't mind."

"Done, and done," he said, cheerfully, and released her hand.

"Fine send-off they're giving the boys," he said, changing his line of conversation, trying to curry her favor. "No wonder so many wanted to join the cavalry with the finest horseflesh around."

He looked at her rather queerly, and asked, "What's Clay going to do with all his horses? Let the Union buy them?"

Surprised, she answered, "I—I don't really know much about that. All I do know is a few of the boys didn't own horses, so the Union is buying them and deducting the amount from their pay. But as far as the rest of the horses, Pa's never discussed the matter with me."

"I see. Of course, both sides will be looking for stock…especially prime stock."

Marnie drew her brows together, and questioned: "What are you trying to say, Duke? That the Confederacy will be coming to Pa to buy horses?"

"No, not in the least," he denied with a tight grin. "I'm just saying that war brings desperate measures…whether North or South."

His rhetoric had Marnie confused. Just what Duke Morgan was getting at, she didn't know but had a sense there was something sinister in the questions he was asking. Much to her relief, Clay was hurrying toward them…a scowl on his face, he didn't bother to hide.

"Here comes Pa, Duke," she said a little nervously, noticing her father took fast long-legged strides, nearly a lope. When her father was riled about something, he didn't hold back his feelings, and she envisioned a quarrel between him and Duke. And on a day like today, that would never do.

"I think we should be getting back, Duke. I only came to the buggy to get a little going-away gift for Ben."

Clay Spencer reached them, and before Marnie knew what was happening, Clay knocked a gun up from a man who immediately shot the pistol in the air.

The crowd heard the shot and a dozen or so men immediately ran toward the scene.

Clay Spencer rammed a hard shoulder into the man's chest as he fought for the pistol. The force of it knocked the man onto the ground and, in falling, he released the gun.

Duke turned at the sound of the shot, and seeing the scuffle taking place, immediately turned pale.

The shooter was Theron Bales, and the shot had been intended for Duke Morgan.

Clay stood looking at Theron for a moment and then extended a hand to help him up.

"Why did you want to shoot him, Theron?" Clay asked, adrenaline still pumping.

Theron reached on the ground for his hat and slapped it against his thigh, disappointed that his effort to kill Duke Morgan had been thwarted by Clay.

Settling the hat back on his head, "I'll tell you why I was going to shoot him," Theron snarled with twisted lips as he addressed the crowd. "I have no sympathy for a man who would malign our boys fighting for the Union. Told me himself they were nothing but a bunch of scalawags a few minutes ago, so I went and got a gun and was going to kill him, I was!"

There was a murmuring among the crowd, and Duke Morgan, opening his mouth to reply, shut it instead, a half-desperate, half-defiant look on his face.

"Is that true?" asked Clay, giving Duke a steady look.

When Duke didn't respond, and with eyes cold as winter rock, Clay said crisply, "I told you that you would end up choosing sides. And to think your own brother, Jim, is one of the enlistees! A scalawag, you say!"

Jim Morgan pushed in, and after a quick glance at him, Duke Morgan turned and gave Clay Spencer a contemplative look of his own. The die was now cast. It was apparent to all that a side had been chosen by Duke…the Confederate side…and without so much as a "Thank you for saving my life" to Clay...Duke, with a stiff face, turned and walked away.

Ben was surrounded by family and allowed his mother to press her lips to his cheek in a kiss, but the last few days had been hard as his mother was never one to disguise her feelings. True, she had kept her silence and no longer badgered him about his enlistment, but she was wounded, he knew, and about that he could do nothing.

"You must be brave, Mother," Ben implored, and his voice changed subtly. It was deeper, with an urgency of impending departure. "You must be brave…for me…and for Father."

Tears filled her eyes as the call came for them to mount.

"I must go," he said, and turned from her and stepped into the saddle.

She clutched his leg and leaned into it. She thought madly: Let the whole of the Union and Confederacy, alike, collapse, but you must not die. No, neither you nor Judah!

She lifted her head and looked at her son that looked so much like Judah and her heart constricted. He smiled faintly and the smile was like Judah's in a younger face.

"Come back to me, Ben," she begged softly with a sob. "Come back to me."

"I will, Mother," he told her, and leaned to pat her on the shoulder. "I promise. I'll be back when you least expect it."

And as the call sounded for formation, he turned and rode away, leaving her hand to fall and grasp nothing but air.

Judah had not departed among cheering crowds as these soldiers were today, but he had left, just the same.

She remembered that first day when Judah and his father rode up to her father's ranch, the day she had first seen him. She felt something then, and it wasn't long until she realized she loved him. A complex person, he was a man that held his feelings close to the vest and did not give himself easily to anything or others, but when he gave, it was with all his heart. There was no in-between about Judah Cross. Just as his commitment to her had been, so, to her detriment, it was with the war.

Why had both he and Benjamin gone, riding off into the war, into a world so unlike what they had both known?

Why had he gone, Judah who was so devoted to home and family, who knew the comforts of good food and soft feather beds? What fare was there for him now? Death awaited him, that fact she felt in the depths of her heart, a gnawing anxiety that grew stronger as time went by. He need not have gone. He was safe, well-off financially, comfortable. But he had gone, leaving her to fend on her own.

Marnie remembered him standing by the carriage when she was leaving *The Crossing*, remembered the look on his face, remembered her lack of encouraging response when he told her good-bye, but merely averted her head in silence as she drove off.

As Company C disappeared into the distance, the crowd that gathered cheered them until the last rider was gone from sight. A few women standing close to her, turned, their faces beaming, casting a wide smile to no one in particular.

She imagined their raised eyebrows should they learn how she really felt, because for her, their cheering was only a reminder that she was now without husband or son.

CHAPTER SEVEN

A FEW WEEKS LATER Marnie was sweeping the house. She entered the parlor that was glaring with harsh sunshine coming from the side windows. Opening the door, she stood there, breathing in the heavy, humid air. "It's going to be like an oven today," she muttered to herself, her hand on her moist neck, "and it's still early morning." Putting the broom aside, she unwound the scarf she had used to keep dust off her hair and threw it on a table.

Wandering to the orchard, hoping a breeze would kick up, Marnie took note the sourwood trees were in blossom. The bees, in profusion, buzzed thickly throughout the white blossoms.

For all of Seth's predictions of bad times to come, she was comforted by the fact they would have an ample supply of honey for sweetening if his calculations came true.

It had been several weeks since she had seen Seth, and she wondered passionately what was keeping him. He was to drive his stock here and every day she watched for him but he never showed. Had the Confederates entered the county and confiscated his horses? And, if so, did he put up a fight, and was he hurt?

Her father hadn't been home for a week either. After driving his stock there, he had been building some type of living quarters in the valley beyond the cave, and forbade her from coming there. She felt listless all morning, with only Mae and Judith for company. Judith was missing her beau Zane Banyon at *The Crossing* and acted just as languid as Marnie.

Another thing was bothering her. She'd had few calls for her medical services since she came back from Stone Valley, and she didn't have any herbs except what Mae had on hand. She treated a woman with basswood blossom tea for her female troubles, and was called to the Harmon home down the road where Bessie was expecting her first child. The calls had not become frequent yet, as they had in the past. Of course, some were new to the area and would not have known her skills, and others had died or moved away in these last twenty years. Did the other doctors leave for enlistments as Judah did, or were they still in town?

She thought about mentioning it to Mae, but Mae had always raucously voiced her opinion about Marnie's wanderings throughout this part of the county tending to sick folk and dispensing her herbs. And what good would it do for anyone to send for her anyway? She had no herbs to dispense.

It had been twenty years since she had been to her herb room. Returning from the orchard and crossing the dogtrot, she opened the door where they had been stored. This was her special room that her father built for her and entering the room, she saw nothing had been touched since her departure to Stone Valley.

Baskets still hung from the ceiling with herbs and roots gathered long ago in them, and the sight of them comforted her. The table was whitened with dust, and she reached for a cloth to wipe the table, and for a few moments, her mind brushed off its memories, and she relived the long ago past of traipsing through these hills, dispensing herbs to sick people. Granny Forbes had taught her everything she knew about herbs before she passed on.

The first memory of Judah going with her on such a call was to the home of Duke Morgan where his uncle lay sick. It was on that trip that Judah first warned her about Duke. Judah saw past his attempt to be charming, even then.

Marnie's heart twisted painfully. Oh, how she missed Judah!

Rubbing her eyes in an attempt to shut her mind to his memory…she then sniffed the air. Was it her imagination? Could she still smell the herbs' earthy fragrance? No. It was merely the mustiness of the room, closed for these past twenty years.

The despair she had felt over Ben's leaving had permeated everything she had done for days. She could not go on like this and instantly decided gathering fresh herbs and roots was what was needed to pick her spirits up, and there was no time like the present to start gathering.

She had taken note of herbs along the way to their earlier trip to the cave. A patch of boneset for fever, Jack-in-the-pulpit for snakebite, basswood blossom for female trouble, golden ginseng, sassafras root, and others.

She untied her apron, grabbed a couple of baskets off a side table, and pulled the door to behind her. She felt almost giddy as though she were stepping back in time to a place where war did not wage, husbands and sons were not killed on the battlefield, leaving behind grieving wives, sisters, sweethearts, and mothers, where life was once simple and uncomplicated.

Clay Spencer might have given orders for her to not venture as far as the cave, but he sure never said she couldn't gather herbs.

The night was alive with movement. Seth McCord stood on his porch, leaning against a post. In the distance, a coyote howled and something scurried in the night.

He hadn't looked at the clock but knew instinctively that morning was not far off. Someone had rustled a couple of his horses before, and he thought a little while ago that he heard a shod hoof touch stone, a saddle's leather creak, and at the sound had pulled on his boots and picked up his rifle, and without lighting a lamp, stepped outside.

The stars alone were still, and on the other side of his property, huge rocks cast their deeper shadow in the brooding darkness, and far away beyond the confines of the porch, a wolf howled.

Seth made the decision at that moment to move his horses today. "Should have done it before now," he thought, "but I had to get some crops in."

He had only one hand on the place to help him and they temporarily stored the root crops in a large hole they had dug and covered them with straw to hide from the Confederates. Normally using the spring house to store his bounty, he dared not risk it now. That would be one of the first places they would look. He just hoped he could transfer most of them to Clay's ranch before anything got to them, especially the potatoes. He may not have much else after the marauders would come through, but as long as he could put a potato on the plate, and have some meal from ground corn to make bread, he was satisfied. His crop of corn was ready for picking, perhaps in a few days he would start. Seth briefly thought some of Clay's help might lend a hand, but, no…he decided…Clay had enough going on at his own place with his own hands joining the ranks.

It was the same story all over Clinton County. The young men were leaving. Some going into the infantry, some into the cavalry, and that meant the farms were short-handed.

The relative peace they had enjoyed since Company C left on August 3rd was only tentative now. Churches were no longer holding services, His own pastor was joining up and closing his services soon, and schools were no longer in session.

"Boss?" sounded a hushed voice in the night.

Seth McCord turned and looked in the direction of the voice, and Ed Farrell stepped into view.

"Ed!" Seth exclaimed, quietly. "You're just like an Indian, sneaking up on me like that."

Ed grinned and Seth could see his white teeth in the faint light of the sickle moon.

A man, two inches under six feet, Ed had wavy red hair, was stocky with muscular arms from hard work.

"I thought I heard something a few moments ago, boss."

"Me too," answered Seth, and turned to look in the darkness again.

The wind rustled, then; as quickly, died away. That was unusual, the wind blowing a short burst early before dawn. Then they heard that sound again—a faint beating of a horse's hooves against the turf.

Ed pulled his rifle up, ready to fire. The rider did not stop, but continued on his way until they no longer heard the steady clip-clop of hooves.

"Think it was more than one rider?" Ed whispered.

"Can't tell for sure," Clay answered. "I hope so. It's too dark to run horses. Just hope no one is camped out there waiting until we are gone."

"You know, boss, when I was down by the county line," Ed told him, "I heard that Union supporters from Overton and Fentress Counties are making their way up through Clinton County. Heard they're headed for Camp Dick Robinson. Hundreds of them are coming through to enlist at Camp Dick Robinson and heard they are all kinds. Old gray-haired men, middle-aged men, and little boys. Could be what we heard were some of them passing through."

"Could be, at that," he agreed.

Seth was quiet for a few minutes, ordering his thoughts. "Ed," he said suddenly, "I'm going to move the horses today."

"I thought you'd be doing that," Ed said. He mulled silently over reports he had heard. "Tell me, boss, if there are sesech about, how are you going to cover the horses' tracks?"

"I've been thinking about that," Seth said thoughtfully. "I believe I'll lead the horses first, and then you drive some cattle behind to mingle over their tracks. I just hope they don't come in and take the chickens and pigs and the rest of the livestock while we are gone, not to mention the crops I have in. Those Reb boys haven't been on the prowl too bad yet, and I'd like to get out of here what I can before they are."

Seth was suddenly restless. Never one to lazy around when there was work to be done, he straightened and said, "Well, it will be light soon. We can't do anything in the dark. You start breakfast and I'll grab a shave."

Ed had bacon frying, and Seth was standing before a small mirror, shaving.

Dishes from the day before were still unwashed, and as Ed tackled enough dishes to set the table with, he fumed, "If I keep washing these dishes, my hands will get as soft as those dress kid gloves you never use that you've got in that top dresser drawer."

With a wet hand, Ed adjusted the ruffled band of the apron that had slipped off his shoulder.

Seth chuckled. He was used to the sight of Ed in an apron since his mother died. They both did the housekeeping, if that was what you could call it. The house hadn't had a good cleaning since she passed. It was hard enough seeing to the farm, much less domestic duties.

"When are you going to get married, boss?" Ed asked as he washed a cup and held it up for inspection. "We could stand having a woman around here to take care of chores."

Seth tilted his head slightly and sighted along his jaw. He drew the razor carefully along it and rinsed it in water. "Me?" he asked, raising the razor to his face again. "What gives you the idea that I'm looking?"

He continued shaving as Ed dried his hands and stepped to the stove to tend to the food.

"Well," he remarked as he removed the bacon, and then broke eggs into the skillet, "I've heard some talk around town."

"Oh, yeah?" Seth stropped his razor. "What kind of talk, and who is doing the talking?"

"Well, you know how it is, boss. One says one thing and one says another."

Razor held in midair, Seth turned to look at him, puzzled. "What are you talking about?"

"Oh...some say you're sweet on Jess Morgan's daughter, and some say you're a confirmed bachelor."

Seth laughed. "What do *you* say?" and went back to shaving.

Ed shrugged his shoulders as he took two plates he just washed and filled them with bacon and set them on the table.

"Me, personally," he remarked quietly, "I think Felicity Morgan would make a fine wife. She's not much on prettiness, grant you, but still, she'd make a fine wife."

Seth touched a place on his jaw he had just nicked. "I agree with you," he said, dabbing the towel to the nick. "She would, indeed...for some man."

"Well, if you want to hear further what I have to say," Ed said mysteriously as he laid down forks, "there is only one girl you've got a hankering for."

Seth finished his shaving and cleaned his razor and brush.

When he didn't answer, Ed said pointedly, "And you know who I'm talking about."

Seth put the razor and brush away and hung his towel on the rack. Seth remained silent.

"Don't act like you don't hear me," Ed softly scolded, and with skillet in hand, deposited eggs swimming in grease on their plates. Returning the skillet to the stove, he threw over his shoulder, "It's that Cross woman, that's who it is. I see how your face lights up when you hear her name."

Ed had been with Seth many years. They had been good years, and there was a rare understanding between them.

"She's married," Seth said offhandedly as he took a seat at the table.

"That doesn't make much difference," Ed said as he poured the coffee, "to some men."

"Maybe not to some men," Seth said dryly and reached for the sugar as Ed removed his apron and threw it over a chair, "but it does to *her*."

Excited that she had already gathered a great bounty, Marnie Cross decided she would ride over to Kara McKendrick's place and have a look for herbs on her way there. On an impulse that she might need it, she retrieved a pistol from her father's office.

Seth was leading his string of horses toward Clay Spencer's place, when he was met by Marnie driving a buggy. A wide-brimmed hat was cinched into place by a chin strap and she was alone.

"What do you think you are doing," he demanded, and drew up sharply in front of her horse, forcing it to stop, "riding out here alone?"

She bristled at his tone. "What I usually do when there's no one around to ride with me."

"Well, I'm around now!" he declared.

"That may be, but you haven't been for some time," she accused, prepared to snap the reins again. "Just where have you been?"

It was on the tip of her tongue to say, *Keeping company with Felicity, I suppose,* but didn't.

"I've been getting crops in, for your information, and haven't had time to socialize."

"Oh," she said, taken down a bit. "I wondered why you hadn't brought the horses yet. I was just going to visit Kara McKendrick."

Without another word, Seth dismounted his horse and climbed onto the seat. "Give me those reins," he ordered brusquely. And before she could reply, he took the reins from her and began to turn the buggy around.

"To restate your own question, what do you think *you* are doing?" she said indignantly, trying to take the reins from him as he turned the horse toward the way she came.

He brushed her hands aside with his arm, and then tugged the horse to halt.

Turning to her, "Don't you know you shouldn't be out in these hills alone?" he said, more as a statement than a question.

"I can manage," she answered, stiffly. "I always have."

"Not now, you can't," was his unsmiling reply.

"You mean to say I'm not capable of protecting myself?" she huffily asked.

"Lady…I mean just that."

Marnie reached down and drew out the pistol she had in a basket by her feet.

"You see?" she triumphantly said and waved it in the air. "I'm armed and can defend myself. Besides," she said loftily, "I don't think anyone would stoop so low as to shoot a woman."

He looked at her incredulously. "Don't count on that. War time is a different time. You never know what people will do."

"Don't be a gander. I'm not afraid. Pa never stopped me from wandering before, even while I was growing up."

"I remember all too well," he said, and wrenched the pistol from her hand, returning it to the basket. "Does Clay know you're gallivanting around today without a chaperon?"

Her blue eyes held a denial. "Well—no, he doesn't, if you must know," she said hesitantly and looked away. "He's been at the cave working on living quarters."

He gave a scolding shake of his head. "Just what I figured. With the possibility that Confederates may be about, I didn't think he would let you run off by yourself."

For one moment she sat, anger swirling inside her. Who was he to take her to task?

Her voice turned indignant. "Pa never gave me any orders to keep to the house before he left!"

"He should have," Seth answered, none too graciously.

Her eyes sparked. "Well, Seth McCord," she said in a prickly tone, "I'm married and no longer your concern."

"You may be married, but you've been my concern since you were young, Marnie." His eyes held hers in challenge, and that look made her lean into her side of the buggy. What was he thinking? Did Seth McCord think just because Judah was no longer around that he would take his place?

"You may not be aware of it," he said, interrupting her thoughts, "but if something happened to you, blood would be shed, and there's enough of that already."

"What do you mean?"

"Just what I said. It's one thing for a man to be killed, quite another for a woman or child, for that is something that would not be tolerated."

She saw the warning and concern in his eyes. With resignation, she lapsed into thought again. Seth was not only looking out for her safety, but for the welfare of the Home Guard, and they were on tenterhooks as it was. If he just wasn't so domineering…treating her as though she was a mindless child!

The cry of bawling cattle was coming from behind and intensified as the moments passed.

She turned toward that sound. "What do I hear?" Marnie was surprised. "Is that cattle?"

Seth opened his mouth in an attempt to continue in the vein of conversation, but thought better of it. "That's right, they are," he said instead.

He handed her the reins and stepped out of the buggy. Looking back, he said, "I don't want these horses to get spooked. Come on, I'm taking them to the cave today and you're going with me. If we meet anybody on the road, let me do the talking."

CHAPTER EIGHT

EVENING WAS DRAWING NEAR at Clay Spencer's ranch home. Seth's horses and cattle had been driven to the valley and anxious to feed the livestock he had left home, sent Ed Farrell on ahead of him.

"Keep that daughter of yours at home," Seth sternly advised Clay Spencer as they stood near the door of Clay's barn. "She doesn't understand the danger of running around alone at this time. It's coming down to it that it might not be safe for even a man to be alone on the road."

Clay frowned, continued with his arranging of bridles hanging on the wall, and then looked sharply at Clay. "I think she knows more than you realize, Seth. She doesn't say much, but the little she does say indicates to me that she's worried."

"She's worried all right, but not about herself." Sarcasm edged Seth's voice. "Do you know what she did this morning when I met her on the road? She produced a pistol from a basket in the buggy." He gave a short laugh and the sound was without mirth. "She thinks all she has to do is wave that gun at someone and they'll run scared. We've got an explosive situation here in Clinton County, Clay, you know that, with some standing for the Confederacy and some for the Union. Everyone is forced to take one side or the other. I know Kentucky has tried to stay neutral in this war, and they can sign all the treaties with the North and South all they want, but that strategy isn't working."

Clay grimaced. "I guess you're right, Seth," he agreed a little sheepishly. "I'm afraid it's my fault. I've always let Marnie have her way since she was a child, and she pays little mind to me now."

"If you put your foot down strong enough, Clay," Seth said, adamantly, "she'll listen."

Clay shook his head. "I don't believe she will. Even though I haven't told her, I've been thinking maybe she needs to take Judith and go back to Stone Valley while trouble is kicking up here, but she's now got it in her mind to doctor the people around here again."

Clay signed deeply as he ran his hand across the back of his neck in frustration. "I don't know, Seth, I guess she'll just have to learn for herself. That's the kind of girl she is and has always been."

Seth shuddered and was silent for a few moments. To think Marnie had to learn the hard way would be devastating. Thoughts began to form in his mind the things that could befall a woman like her. It so distressed him that he dismissed the deliberations immediately from his mind.

"I tried to watch out for her when she was growing up," Seth finally said, looking out the door and watched Marnie milling about the dogtrot with herbs she had gathered on their trip to the valley, "but I can't always be there for her now.

"I've had word," he said, turning back to Clay, "that a Confederate camp has been set up across the border near Travisville in Fentress County. They refer to it as Camp McGinniss. Some in Clinton County are calling it McGinniss Sesech Camp.

"It's rumored there is a regiment there they call the "Bull Pups." It's told they are convicts from the Nashville Penitentiary pardoned on condition they enlist in the Confederate Army. I hear they are a rough bunch.

"Not only that, but Captain Willis Scott Bledsoe is organizing a rebel guerrilla company there. It will be one thing to deal with soldiers and quite another to deal with guerrillas."

"Guerrillas? Tell me, Seth," questioned Clay, "how is it that you know so much about what is going to happen?"

Seth ran his finger over the bridge of his nose in thought. "Just things I hear. Think about it, Clay. These mountain boys are rough men. They have lived free, roaming wherever they wanted. Some won't take easy to military training. So, as I see it, there are some, most likely, will join up with guerrilla bands, and it's going to be a bad time for us all that support the Union.

"By the way," Seth continued, "did you hear about Duke Morgan?"

"I heard something about an arrest, but don't know what came of it."

"That's right. It was across the line in Fentress County. He was arrested by Union sympathizers down there. They were going to take him to Camp Dick Robinson for trial…for what, exactly, I don't know."

Seth laughed dryly. "Wouldn't you know it? He escaped. Now he has declared war on all Union supporters. Hear he is moving his family to White County, Tennessee."

"He's a bad sort," Clay agreed. "I've tried to tell Marnie that."

"Well, yes…I've done the same.

"Keep some supplies," Seth added, "and a couple of cows here, perhaps a few chickens, for if you don't, they will get suspicious and wonder where you are hiding your stock and food. As it is, you'll have a hard time explaining the absence of what we've driven there…to anyone who knows you, that is. I'm not saying you'll be able to hold onto your provisions here, but stay in your home until necessary to leave. I doubt if they will burn it, but, then again, you never know. And if I were you, I'd keep my saddle horses picketed in the woods. Ed and I are doing the same."

CHAPTER NINE

MARNIE STOOD before the long pier glass, surveying her violet watered-silk dress with its yards of material over her hoops, reflecting her violet eyes, and twisted herself from side to side and hiking her skirt up a bit, smiling at the matching flat-heeled violet slippers. Her blond hair was fastened in curls on her head instead of its usual chignon, and she curtsied to the mirror, responding to a request by an imaginary partner for a dance. She laughed at herself, giving her curls a little shake.

She felt she was back again, before the war began, before Judah and Benjamin went away, when life was pleasant, indeed, the dutiful, helpful wife of Judah Cross in his role as a doctor. Presiding over balls and dances at the hotel while her father's brother Cole was in charge of running the hotel itself. Served on bazaars and committees of the church. Yes…life was good then.

Judge Hardin's daughter, Cadence, was to be wed at his home in Albany, and in spite of talk of war hovering at the borders of Clinton County, Cadence insisted on a fancy wedding. Her fiancé, Jeremiah Thornton was enlisting with the Union Army and leaving in a week's time, and Marnie, with an unexpected spark of excitement, was looking forward to attending. There had been precious few social diversions, with only a few hasty marriages performed before Company C had left, and they had been small placid affairs.

Marnie threw open the shutters and looked outside. It was a beautiful day, fitting for such a wedding and the prospect of dancing once again. Outside her window, the mockingbirds were voicing their multi-sounded songs, and at their singing, her thoughts turned again to the balls she attended at their resort in Adair County. Patrons came from near and far to stay at the hotel and partake of the mineral waters. Grand, the hotel was, and many evenings she had spent there, dancing and playing hostess to its varied guests.

A small frown drew her brow as she thought of the many elegant dresses in her wardrobe at *The Crossing*. This particular dress, one of her favorites, was among those she had packed to bring with her. As a matter-of-fact, Judah had favored this dress among all her finery. It was as though something within her wanted to retain in her memory the splendor of the years she'd had with Judah, something lost, she feared, that may not be regained.

Most in the county did not own such finery as this and she hesitated wearing it. She usually dressed without her hoops since she arrived to stay with her father for it was quite inconvenient searching for herbs in the countryside and attending to anyone who called for her medical services.

"Perhaps this dress is too elegant, but," she reasoned, inspecting her image closer in the mirror, "this is a wedding and there are precious few reasons anymore for such a gala."

As Clay was to accompany her and Judith today, she hoped that he would refrain from talking about matters of war. He talked about it morning, noon and night, as well as all the men he came in contact with. Goodness! They acted like the war was something sacred and that everyone should bow down at the altar to!

Coming home to Clinton County was not what she expected she had to admit to herself. The men and women looked the same as she had known them while growing up, but they were different now. They lived on the edge as everything in their world was changing. This was what life was like for her father and the men—never quite comfortable or safe, always with a trace of danger. But they reveled in it, as though some type of camaraderie knit them together.

As for herself, she was holding onto life as she had known it, pleasantries and caring for those whom called for her services in spite of voices she heard around her. Maybe she had laid the hourglass on its side to keep the sand from running…perhaps she was ignoring the death knell that was sounding in spite of her indifference…but for her, it was her way of keeping her sanity.

"Today", she said out loud decidedly to her reflection in the mirror, "is a day to leave behind worry and hurt and thoughts of battlefields and war."

Marnie smothered a smile. Of a sudden, it was no longer wartime. For her, she was back again in Adair County at *The Crossing*, the wife of Doctor Judah Cross, daughter of Clay Spencer, and granddaughter of Judge Sam and Rachel Spencer. She was going to a wedding, and before the day was over would dance the afternoon away.

She was brought up short, remembering that married men, as a rule, did not seek out other women than their wives to dance with. Then she remembered, she was now in Clinton County and many men had been leaving to join the war, and no doubt, she would not lack for company with their wives. Being the sociable creature that she was, that would serve just as well.

Squaring her shoulders and pulling on her gloves, she felt better now than she had since leaving *The Crossing* and opened the door with a pleased smile.

CHAPTER TEN

IN THE PARLOR of Judge Hardin's home, amid the blaze of candles, Cadence Hardin, in her white-satin wedding gown, her face glowing, became Cadence Thornton. Jeremiah stood proudly in his uniform, and an unbidden thought slipped into Marnie's consciousness as to whether he would survive the war or not. Quickly, she shut the thought out lest it become, by some circumstance, a reality. It would not do to think such a thought in light of the happiness radiating on Cadence's face.

She was here to have a good time and excitement flamed her heart again at seeing so many people, the strain of war absent from their faces, and, to Marnie, it seemed as though those present had set aside for the day, thoughts of husbands, sons, and fathers that were gone. Although the crowd was conspicuously lacking young and middle-aged marriageable men, there was a gaiety about the women in attendance that caught her up in its current in spite of the fact that many she did not recognize, as she had been gone from the county a long time.

In searching the crowd, she saw Seth McCord flanked by several eligible young ladies, all vying for his attention, and all a mite too young for him. One in particular stood out to her. She had on a gray organdie dress, with its blue-colored satin sash, light brown hair knotted at the neck. But it was not the dress, nor the hair that arrested her attention. It was the look on the girl's face that radiated in her soft brown eyes. There was no mistaking that gaze. She was in love with Seth…utterly.

"Could this be Felicity Morgan?" Marnie wondered with a pang. "The girl that everyone speculates would soon become engaged to Seth McCord?"

The parlor had been cleared of furniture and musicians were tuning up for the dance by the twang of fiddles heard. The floor was waxed and polished awaiting dancing feet and swishing skirts. In the dining room beyond, Mrs. Hardin was presiding over a heavy mahogany table laden with fried chicken and venison, buttered roasting ears, peas, assorted breads, pies, and her favorite…apple cake. A door opened off the dining room to the side yard where tables were adorned with white tablecloths for the guests when they wished to dine.

Judith, who had been stationed by Marnie's side, made her way to friends she had made after coming to Clinton County, leaving her mother alone.

Noticing Marnie bereft of company, and with a sudden lift of his eyebrows, Seth disengaged himself from his small company of female admirers and made his way, striding casually to her side.

"I didn't know you were coming to the wedding today," remarked Marnie, surprise sounding in her voice. "What are you doing here?"

"Didn't you know that I show up in the most unexpected places?" Seth bantered.

"Even weddings?" she returned. "I thought you stayed away from such gatherings."

"I have nothing against weddings…as long as they're someone else's," he replied with a good-natured smile.

Felicity Morgan was casting a look their way, a look that was not entirely lost on Marnie. It was a bit of a woe-be-gone stare, and Marnie wondered if Seth had any idea of the love that Felicity plainly had for him.

"Probably not," she thought and turning her attention back to him, Marnie said, "I suppose that means you're not the marrying kind."

"Not necessarily," he finally answered, amused at her probing. "If it's to the right person, well, that's a different matter."

Heedless of the crowd, Seth perused her in a way that brought a flush to her face, and she wished she had brought her fan to hide behind, if only to forestall any gossip springing up about them. It bothered her in a way that he was so open about his feelings for her. And her father, to her distress, seemed to encourage Seth in his importune advances. Not that he believed in divorce, but Clay had never hidden his approval of Seth and his displeasure of Judah. Yet, as Judah had become so successful in life, Clay's unbending attitude was perplexing to her. And as it seemed that Clay was holding firm to his feelings, Judah and Marnie did not visit Clinton County.

"You are particularly enchanting today...especially in that dress,"

"Fitting for the occasion, wouldn't you say?" she answered flippantly, trying to hide her embarrassment.

He smiled a knowing smile as Felicity made her way toward them. "Very fitting," He turned to Felicity. "Wouldn't you say so, Felicity?"

"How's that, Seth?" a questioning look in Felicity's eyes.

"I said that Marnie looks very fitting in that dress."

Marnie was taken aback, but the obvious statement to Felicity was meant to deter any designs she had on Seth.

Felicity said very quietly, "Oh, yes. Mrs. Cross is quite beautiful."

Once again, Seth was embarrassing her and Marnie felt caught in the crossfire. It was one thing to make such a comment, but to treat Felicity so cruelly?

As the music began playing a reel, Marnie poised herself to move into Seth's arms at the invitation in his eyes.

However, Seth reached out for Felicity's hand instead. "Will you dance with me, Felicity?" he asked.

Surprise sketched across her face and elation washed through Felicity. Her eyes lit, revealing her heart, and she eagerly reached for his hand.

They moved off together, and Seth threw Marnie a half-smile, a glimmer of satisfaction shining on his face as they stepped into the crowd of dancers. Marnie looked into his unreadable face in confusion and took a step back. What kind of game was Seth playing? Was he trying to make her jealous? And if so, why?

The slight stung and something rose up in Marnie as she watched them dance, something she did not like and tried to analyze. She felt wounded, wounded by the slight Seth had given her and she didn't know why, yet common sense told her friendship was all she could offer—or receive. Because of marriage to Judah, first and foremost.

The day which started out very promising had quickly turned around as a flock of birds in the air, changing course at a second's notice. That's exactly what she wanted to do…like a child, turn and fly away home.

Marnie glanced out the door to the side yard. Where it had started out a bright sunny day, it suddenly felt as though the sun was shut out of her life. And for the first time since she returned to Clinton County, she wanted to go home. Not home to her father's house…to Clay Spencer's home, but…

Home…to The Crossing. To a place she was the mistress of. A place where her word was obeyed.

Home to *The Crossing*? "This is ridiculous. Whatever is the matter with me?" she thought, taking herself to task in her chaos of thoughts. Mulling over the incident, she tried to convince herself she was making too much of the episode, yet it left her in a questionable muddle.

She turned, almost stumbled, in confusion to the refreshment table and automatically smiled at Mrs. Hardin, murmuring "Thank you" to cake and cider offered, adding her congratulations of the marriage of her daughter. At least she still had the presence of mind to be courteous.

It was a very warm day, as August tended to be, and looking beyond Mrs. Hardin, she ventured outside, looking for a place to sit.

At one table sat her father blustering on about something or other concerning Confederate sympathizers in the county to some of the men gathered about him there, and she glared at him. Her angry look did no good, however, for he didn't realize that she was there, so intent was he in conversation.

Few guests were outside and Marnie chose a table far from the ramblings of her father and his companions.

The air was still and she wished for the second time that day that she had brought her fan. Any well-dressed lady at such a function always carried a fan…at least in New Wellington.

She picked at her cake in thought, absently swatted at a fly with her fork, unaware the music had stopped. And before she knew what was happening, was besieged by her daughter, cheeks flushed, and smiling from ear to ear.

"Oh, Mother," Judith said breathlessly, hugging her mother, and then wiped her forehead with her handkerchief. "It's been so long since I've danced. It was absolutely wonderful!"

Marnie gave her daughter a smile which didn't quite reach her eyes. She really had neglected her as of late, leaving her to Mae's care, so involved was she in tending the sick. The thought had not entered her mind the past few weeks that Judith might be lonely. She thought she had adjusted being away from Zane Banyon at *The Crossing*. She was such a good-natured girl. It was not in her to complain.

"I'm glad you're having a good time, Judith," she said, giving her a hug again. "I just wish there were more young men here for you to dance with."

Judith rambled on for a moment, and then dashed off for refreshments. Seth stepped through the door and approached the table where Marnie was deep in thought. The music had started again, playing a waltz this time.

CHAPTER ELEVEN

"…PARTIAL TO WALZES."

Her musings evaporated and she looked at Seth. "You were saying?"

"I said, 'If I remember correctly, you were partial to waltzes.'"

Marnie turned her head toward the music, suddenly aware of the tempo.

Their eyes locked, his giving her a questioning look, and hers skittering away toward the house.

"That's right. I am. I am, indeed."

"Well, then," he said expectantly, "shall we?"

She debated whether to favor him with a dance or not, but not wanting to create a disturbance, rose, and took his extended hand with her own limp one, and allowed him to lead her inside. Across the threshold she moved into his arms, yet she didn't have the mind for it.

Color seeped into her cheeks at his scrutiny.

"It's obvious that you're struggling about something," he informed her after they had danced around the room twice. When she looked into his eyes with surprise, he asked, "Want to tell me about it?"

"I—I—" she began, her reluctance plain. She didn't like making a scene, especially in such a large crowd. To unburden herself here, on Cadence's wedding day, was not the proper place. It was obvious

Seth, self-assured that he was, thought nothing of such civility or he would have waited until a more appropriate time and place to question her.

She tamped down unspoken words—words that wanted answers. "It's nothing," she stated, glancing quickly around to see if they had been overheard. She tried to smile, but it fell far short.

He stopped dancing, eyed her thoughtfully and, casting his eye on the door, the yard, and guests beyond, suggested, "Come outside. You don't have the heart for this today."

Feeling awkward that he sensed her mood, and that others looked at them questionably when they interrupted the flow of the dancers by standing still, she followed him to a corner of the yard, past where her fathers and others were debating the merits of war, to where an empty bench was under an Elm tree. Bidding her to sit, he followed suit.

"Now… What is it that lays so heavy on your mind?"

She hesitated, unsure of him, and she drew a deep breath as if steeling herself against what his reaction would be and what he would say. Perhaps she should keep her thoughts to herself, but she was never one to do so. If something bothered her, she wanted to talk about it, get it out in the open…have the matter settled. Her father told her on more than one occasion that she thought like a man. However a man thought, she did not know. But she knew her own mind, and right now she wanted to get the straight of the matter.

"Go on," he said, after a few moments. "You know you can tell me anything."

"Oh, Seth, I just feel so terrible," she cried quietly, her thoughts tumbled, "and I don't know why."

"Well, why don't you tell me when the feeling started?"

"You'll think I'm silly—or something worse," she confessed reluctantly.

He studied her thoughtfully. "Tell me and let me make up my own mind about it."

“Well,” she began, unable to meet Seth’s probing gaze, feigning a calm she didn’t feel. “I don’t understand, but when you asked Felicity to dance instead of me, it bothered me terribly. And for the life of me, I can’t figure out why.”

“Ah, yes,” he said quietly. “I saw the look on your face, and it was apparent you weren’t pleased.”

Bemused, a half-smile pulled at his mouth. “Could it be that you were a wee bit jealous?” he asked, mocking her words of a few weeks ago.

Her mouth flew open and what crossed her lips rang like a whip. “How dare you, Seth McCord!” She gathered her skirts to rise and show him her back as she walked away.

Immediately he regretted his last remark and instantly, he was on his feet bending over her and pushed her back onto the bench.

“Come now, Marnie,” he said, trying to mollify her. “Compose yourself. You don’t want to give rise to gossip, do you?”

As if he cares, she thought.

“What I do is my affair,” she stated coldly, staring at the ground.

Seth studied her and wondered just how much he should divulge to her. She was so difficult to handle that it was a struggle to keep the upper hand with her. In the end, he decided an impasse like this needed diplomacy…a diplomacy that revealed his feelings, or at least part of them.

“Don’t you really know why I’m here today?” he asked softly.

“It doesn’t really matter to me why you’re here,” she said, trying to be coldly dignified.

“But I suppose to see Felicity,” Marnie finally relented.

“Oh, is that what you think?” Seth answered, making an airy gesture.

When she did not reply, he continued.

“I came because of you,” he said bluntly and his hands jammed in hard fists in his pockets. And as she searched his face, he told her, “You and I are friends—very old and intimate friends. And as Judah is not here, I feel honor-bound to protect you. I’ve told you how bad this war will get, and I would never forgive myself if you should—”

He turned from her, annoyed that he had nearly shown his heart…again.

“I—I’m sorry, Seth,” she said, putting a hand on his arm. “I guess I just didn’t realize.”

He removed his hands from his pockets and said, “No…you never do.”

“I—I just wanted some answers. You know me…how I am.”

“Yes, I know,” he said, and sat down again.

Seth lowered his head in thought for a while and her nerves were on tiptoe, waiting for him to speak.

Then as if a light shined in his understanding, he said contemplatively, “The way I see it, you expected me to ask you, and when I didn’t, you felt rejected.”

Marnie stared at him as if she had not grasped his meaning. “But why in the world would I feel that way? You’re not married and are free to dance with whomever you wish to.”

“Because,” and he rose and paced as though movement gave clarity to his thoughts, and there was agitation in his steps as he drew from a well of thinking rarely visited, “you feel that Judah rejected you when he went away, and when I chose Felicity, it stirred up those same feelings again.”

Eyes wide with wonderment, it suddenly made sense to her. She felt an inexplicable rush of relief wash over her at those words and collapsed against the back of the bench. She wasn’t crazy, after all.

“How—how did you arrive at that conclusion?” she asked, her voice nearly a whisper.

Seth drew up his knee and positioned his foot on the bench, looking down at her, a knowing light in his eyes. “Marnie, dear—it was easy to figure out. You wear your heart on your sleeve where Judah is concerned. Sometimes when you aren’t conscious that anyone is looking at you, you look incredibly sad.”

She gave a shaky smile. “Is it that obvious?”

His eyes looked at her, but through her, past her, looking back at another time. She should have been his. Her children would have been his children, her father his father-in-law. Yet he was far from realizing a relationship with her. And like a fly in the ointment, the one standing between them was Judah. He had watched her leave Clinton County after she married, fighting his anguish, wanting to go after her. So many things he had wanted to tell her but the opportunity was past! Though she had gone, she had never left his heart. Did she truly know the knot of emotion that he was entangled with when he looked at her? In all honestly, he had to admit that he didn't think she did.

"It is." Seth smiled faintly at her question, coming back to the present, but spoke gruffly, as if unwilling to reveal his frustration, keeping the wistfulness from his voice, and he wondered if it was always the way of a man to want what he could not have.

CHAPTER TWELVE

AN URGENT pounding on the door sounded, and as it continued, the music stopped, skirts swishing in dancing, swayed and finally stilled.

Judge Hardin answered the door while others looked on, and the small group of Home Guard filed in from the yard, inquisitive about the commotion.

There, in the doorway, stood two men, which promptly pushed their way through the door, past the judge and turned to face him.

The first thought that entered Judge Hardin's mind, "Somebody's house must have caught fire."

"Judge," addressed one of the men, fair-headed, tall, and the other, about five feet ten inches tall with light hair, blue eyes, and fair skin. "I don't know if you remember me, although I've seen you. I am Ezekiel Chandler, recently moved to Clinton County from Tennessee. This man with me is Ansel Hamilton. He and his family have moved up from Tennessee taking refuge in a house on my property."

"That's fine, Mr. Chandler. But what is it I can do for you gentlemen?"

Chandler stood hat in hand, turning it around. "Well, sir, maybe we were wrong in busting in on you like this, having a party and all, but we were looking for the Home Guard and were told they were here."

“They are indeed. Is there something I can help you with?”

“If I can talk to the Home Guard, please, sir?”

Clay came forward, anticipating trouble, eyes alive with excitement. “We’re the Home Guard if you’d like to step outside,” pointing to the side door.

Marnie sat on the bench, listening to their conversation.

Ansel Hamilton addressed himself to Clay after introductions. “As you well know, Mr. Spencer, Northern Tennessee is divided in its loyalties.

I, as well as Ezekiel here, are from Overton County and are joining Company C for the Union. We have many kinfolk who are divided as well. My cousin, Noble Hamilton has been commissioned a colonel for the Confederacy, and as we feared for our lives, we left hurriedly for Clinton County. My cousin seized my property and placed a lock on the door. Now…that house and its contents are rightly mine. I’m not worried about the house until the war is over, but I find it is necessary to get my furniture and other possessions out of my house. I’d like the Home Guard to go with us.”

There was a general murmuring among the men, and then a nodding in the affirmative.

“All right,” Clay said. “We’ll leave tonight if that’s all right with you.”

“And that,” thought Marnie indignantly, “is the end to a beautiful reception.”

Since the arrival of Ansel and Ezekiel had essentially thrown a damper on the dancing, a general leave-taking was taking place by the guests.

Clay hurried Marnie and Judith into the buggy. Could Clay be right? she thought, as the buggy left faster than their arrival had been. Is war truly coming to Clinton County? War had always seemed in some far off distant land to her where Judah and Benjamin would fight. For the first time since coming home, the realization of war on the home-front hit her and she shivered. It could truly come to their own front door.

It became all so real to her, that fear overcame reason and her heart began to beat faster. They were so close to the border. Could it be that Confederates soldiers were already on the march in the county?

This was the first foray of any Union supporter to cross the Tennessee/Kentucky border…at least that Marnie knew of, and her father was venturing into enemy territory for what, of all things? A bunch of furniture? And none of it his own at that!

For the life of her, she couldn't understand the priorities these men had. It was as though they were egging on aggression, taunting the enemy for a fight, and as she and Judith followed in the buggy behind her father riding on horseback, the reins in her hands became taut until the horse responded in kind. She loosened her grip, giving him his head, trying to calm her fright.

"Mother?" asked Judith, some of the tension in Marnie reflected on her own face.

Marnie, at once realizing her state, forced calmness into her voice and tried to talk of inconsequential things. The wedding, dresses, who had come with whom. And all the while, she was thinking of the valley and making their escape there.

"It's all right, Mother," Judith said softly. "I know it's frightening."

She ventured a glance at Judith. How could her daughter be so calm in the face of impending trouble? Marnie relapsed into silence at Judith's quotation.

"Yea, though I walk through the valley of shadow of death, I will fear no evil. Thy rod and thy staff, they comfort me."

How so like Judah she was, echoing his own words of the Bible! He would be proud of her, of her courage and faith. And it was at this exact moment in the glaring afternoon sun that Marnie determined to somehow find a way to send Judith back to Adair County. Marnie would face the dangers here, but not her daughter…never her daughter! Her husband and son may be gone, but she resolved that no harm would come to her only girl.

The next day, Marnie stayed close to the house. The fact that there was considerable unrest across the border between Union and Confederates supporters had her on tenterhooks…that, and the fact that her father's proposed incursion could cause his death.

Clay Spencer's home was a mere three miles from the county line, and the fact that her father would venture into Overton County on a mission to rescue furniture and household goods was utterly preposterous to her, but Clay, an eager volunteer for such a foolish mission, turned a deaf ear to her pleas to stay home.

"Pa, you just can't go across the border," she had cried, looking up at him on horseback as she leaned against his leg, and for a few moments her mind leaped about for she was back at *The Crossing*, pleading with Judah to not leave her. What price was this trouble exacting from her? Was she losing all the men in her life?

Marnie turned to look at Seth, but he did not look at her or speak. Of a sudden, hate choked all utterance. Clay listened to Seth and was responding to his approval of the action they were taking. She knew her father would stay if Seth would advise, yet he heartily concurred to this mad trip they were taking. Maybe they took her display of emotion for feminine weakness. But she didn't care!

With a pat on her shoulder and a reassuring smile, Clay left, mounted on his horse as Seth drove a wagon pulled by a team of horses to traverse into territory controlled by Colonel Noble Hamilton and his militia regiment.

She nearly laughed out loud at the thought that Seth McCord was a prominent figure of the party. Seth! Always so level-headed! Risking his neck for dishes and furniture! What had the world come to when men debased themselves to such a level as this? Why had they gone, stepping off into the dark, where at the end of the road was death? Where was the grand talk now from orators about the preserving the Union? Where was the roll of drums, rallying men into what they called 'their duty to take up arms'? Patriotism, bah!

Grumbling to Mae did no good. She merely threw her hands in the air and answered, "What do I know?"

Ed Farrell stayed close about the place while Clay and Seth were gone. Marnie heckled him so often about riding over to the border for any news that he made himself scarce and that only added to her irritation.

Throughout the day, for at least a dozen times, Marnie ambled out onto the porch, her eyes peering down the drive for any sign that they had returned. Finally Marnie decided she would saddle her horse and ride to, and, if need be, across the border, for it was easier to go than to wait. Once she was there, she would face the issues as they developed.

She walked back inside, headed for her bedroom and dressed quickly, went to the kitchen and packed a little food and began to fill a canteen with water.

Mae walked in from hanging clothes up in the back yard and taking note of Marnie, questioned, "What are you up to?"

"Just never you mind what I'm up to."

"Well, it sure looks like you're up to something you shouldn't be. Where are you going?"

"If you must know, I'm headed to the border to find out any news about Pa."

And with that said, she ran out the door.

Ed was forking hay into a manger when Marnie walked into the barn.

She worked swiftly, saddling her horse, ignoring him when he suddenly straightened up.

"What are you doing, Marnie?"

She turned, then averted her head and went back to the task of heisting the saddle.

"I'm doing what I should have done in the first place. I'm going to see what's happened to Pa."

"I wouldn't do that, if I were you," he suggested in a quiet tone.

"Yes, it's apparent you wouldn't, but I'm not you."

"Clay said you were to stay here," he argued.

"I know what Pa said," she said and made an impatient gesture, "but I will do what I must."

He looked at her sharply. Now, what did she think she was going to do about it if she found him? She wasn't even carrying a pistol. This girl definitely had a mind of her own, though he thought her mighty foolish. He guessed that was why Seth was drawn to her, but for the life of him, he didn't know why. Women shouldn't act that way, in his opinion. They should be more submissive. He didn't know how her husband handled her, but he guessed he must be a mighty strong man to keep her in line.

But he had been thinking the same thing as she about Clay, Seth, and the rest of the men. Silently, he had agreed with Marnie. Furniture was no reason to be heading into Confederate Territory. To fight a battle, yes...but not for furniture.

Clay and Seth would both have his head for what he was about to do, but if he didn't, he'd be in worse trouble if something happened to Marnie out on her own.

"All right," said Ed, resignation heavy in his voice, and he pulled his watch out of his pocket and clicked it open. It was early afternoon already. "I shouldn't, you know," clicking the watch shut and depositing it back in his pocket. "Clay wanted me to stay here to watch over things, but I'll ride over to see if there's any news if that will keep you home."

Ed saddled his horse, checked his guns, and stepped into the saddle.

He settled his hat on his head and she handed the food and canteen to him.

"Take care of yourself, Ed," she admonished softly, laying a hand on the horse's mane.

"Will do," he answered, and rode out the corral and down the drive.

Appreciation swelled in her breast for what he was doing. He was a top hand, in her opinion. He will go as far as necessary to find Clay, even across the border. That she instinctively knew.

With relief, Marnie watched him go. At least now she would know.

Reining his horse into the trees, Ed Farrell drew up and waited. Had he been seen? If so, would the rider come on?

The rider came on…studying the woods. Ed waited, loosening his gun in the holster. He had crossed the border, moved into enemy territory. Yet, there were still Union residents in the area and he didn't know if the rider was friend or foe.

The rider passed by slowly, cautious of what the woodland might shield and Ed got a good look at his face. Wha—? Duke Morgan! What was he doing riding alone? Duke had been arrested by a party of Union sympathizers, intending to take him Camp Dick Robinson for trial, yet he had escaped and declared open warfare on any Union man.

It was apparent he was headed towards the border. But beyond the direction he was moving, Ed couldn't tell his destination.

From what he had heard, Duke Morgan now went heavily armed. Was he in trouble? Perhaps he decided to high-tail it back into Kentucky. With that thought, he wanted to spit on the ground contemptuously for he never did think much of Duke even though he and Seth were friends of a sort. To him, Duke had always been trouble in the making.

Ed waited until he was out of sight, and then rode out of the shadows into the road.

The day was warm, the sky clear, and the smell was of musky forest. Clay and the others should have arrived at the Hamilton home-place by now, loaded the wagon, and started back, barring any mishap.

Just before dusk Ed came upon Seth furiously driving the wagon loaded with furniture as though a horde of elephants were after him.

Seth jerked on the reins, sawed savagely at the horse's mouth when he met with Ed.

"They could use you back there," Seth said hurriedly, motioning over his shoulder.

"What's happened?"

"We busted the lock on the door and got in. After we were loaded up, we started back. But I guess some Confederate sympathizer got the word to Noble Hamilton, and he rode in with his regiment. Crazy idiot thought he was Napoleon or something, and he came charging ahead of his men, waving his sword at us, telling us to surrender.

"One of our party shot him. I don't know who, but Hamilton fell right off his horse…dead. Clay told me to head for the border with this stuff while they held the regiment off."

"All right," Ed answered through a push of air, wheeled his horse around and raced toward Clinton County's Home Guard. He had never been in a skirmish before, and with heart pounding, every muscle in his body was taut in expectation of a fight.

When Ed departed and Seth started down the road, it suddenly occurred to him that Ed was supposed to be at Clay's place. He wondered if there was trouble at home and decided if there were, Ed would have spoken of it right away.

Marnie. No doubt she had something to do with this.

"*Now,* what has she done?" he wondered and shook the reins as he clicked to the horses.

After Ed had traveled about three miles, he was met with the Home Guard, and seeing him, they halted.

"What are you doing here?" Clay demanded.

"I had to come," Ed stated almost sheepishly. "Marnie was saddling her horse to come after you. It was either me or her and I knew you'd have my head if I had let her come."

Clay shook his head and frowned, and again he thought for the hundredth time that she had need of a mother while growing up. He had always given her a free rein, never been strict with her, and admitted to himself that he never would be. In fact, he admired her spirit as she was never one to shrink from taking the reins of a situation. It was near impossible to hold her back.

"That's just like her," he said with an air of acceptance.

"Well, come on, Ed," Clay said and waved the company forward. "Their regiment scattered and we're making our getaway."

CHAPTER THIRTEEN

SEPTEMBER BROUGHT a change to Albany…a change that foretold things to come, although few fully realized what lay over the horizon. While the residents of Clinton County went about the task of working their farms and making a living, a war wind was in the making where Duke Morgan was concerned. Duke had declared war on any Union supporter, and Clinton County had many.

Most knew he had moved his family to White County after his arrest, and though he still had his farm in Clinton County, people thought erroneously he was gone for good.

On a sunny afternoon, Duke rode into Albany in the company of ten armed rebels, and not one person who saw them pass doubted that trouble was impending. They rode brazenly past the courthouse and sheriff's office, rifles in hand, ready to offer resistance to any man that dared deter them from their preplanned incursion.

A woman went along the walk, holding a child by the hand. At the ferocious look of the band, she pulled the child into the nearest door. Several men were milling about and were brought up short at the unexpected visit of Duke and his men. No one had an inkling that he was coming. There was no time to call the Home Guard in from the county, and no one dared, on his own, confront Duke. Perhaps if Duke was alone, they might have, but in the company of such vicious looking men….

The wind whipped up a little dust in the sun-lit street, and several horses stood three-legged at hitching rails as well as buggies.

Looking carefully around, they promptly stopped at Niland's store and dismounted.

Daniel Niland heard the scraping of boots on the walk indicating several people, and laying aside the task of unpacking a crate, prepared to leave the back room.

"Niland!" called out Duke Morgan.

Daniel Niland entered the store, stopped, mystified at Morgan's band of men, and knew immediately there was trouble afoot.

"Something I can do for you, Duke?" he asked, after his initial shock.

"Yeah," replied Morgan with a grin. "We're here to relieve you of your stock."

"Fine," replied Niland, trying to buoy his expression, and walked behind the counter.

Taking the pencil from behind his ear, Niland grabbed a sheet of paper, and said, "I have some very good merchandise, if you'll just tell me what you need."

Someone closed the door as a woman prepared to enter. She took a quick look inside the window, saw Duke and his men, then turned and hurriedly made her way down the walk as the street soon emptied of people.

"You won't need a pencil and paper for what we want," Duke instructed Niland.

"I'm afraid I don't understand," Niland said, and stiffened ever so slightly, noticing the long bladed knife in his belt. "You *do* want to purchase some goods today, do you not?"

Morgan considered the question, turned to the other men and they all gave a laugh.

"Not purchase," he said, turning back to Niland.

"But—"

"Let's just say, we'll just be *taking* your merchandise."

Duke Morgan gave another laugh. “Charge it to the Clinton County Home Guard.”

At that, the men guffawed as it was known that Niland was one of the Home Guard.

Niland started to protest, and he thought to bring up his pistol from under the counter, but common sense intervened. There was no way he alone could defend his stock against Duke and his men. And from the look in Duke’s eyes, he would not hesitate to shoot him, and Niland was not ready to die.

Moving back against the wall, where they could see him in plain view, Niland’s empty hands clearly visible, they loaded into the wagon with them approximately $2,000.00 worth of merchandise.

The last of the goods in the wagon, Duke lingered a moment, taking one last look around the store. He looked at Niland, bedeviled amusement in his eyes and felt no compassion. He thought, in his opinion, that Niland should consider himself lucky that he didn’t burn the store down. With a snort, Duke Morgan turned on his heel and walked out the door, and untying the reins, mounted his horse and gave the command to leave.

Niland’s eyes followed where Duke’s previously had been. His shelves were now empty, tables devoid of merchandise. What would he do now? He had spent years building up his inventory. How would he support his family? He walked to the open door, and with impotent rage, watched his livelihood disappear down the street as they drove at a rapid click.

Contrary to what had happened at Daniel Niland’s store, some of the Unionist folk of Clinton County still refused to believe that war would come to their county. Some speculated it was a personal feud between Daniel Niland and Duke Morgan.

Their perception of his threat was dismissed by some until….

Duke Morgan and his band of guerrillas began relieving the citizens of Clinton County of their stock of horses and mules and other livestock.

It didn't take long for citizens to realize that if they were to retain their stock, they had to take action. Horses were hidden in woods, in caves, sometimes in cellars to keep them from being stolen.

Seth was very late in leaving. Several men had arrived, and with Seth McCord and Clay Spencer, held a secret meeting in Clay's office.

Marnie had not been apprised of any meeting taking place, and, being naturally inquisitive, kept her ear to the office door, but the muffled words were not to be understood. When finally the door was opened by her father, she, in the act of being discovered, was speechless and blushed in embarrassment at being caught in such a childish deed.

Expecting her father to scold her, she was disarmed by his slow smile at her curiosity as he pinched her cheek, calling her "nosy". Marnie laughed then, easy as a girl, and moved to the side, allowing the men to exit the room. Each man spoke farewell to her, donning their hats as they did so, all but one. Seth McCord…and his look was anything but a look of fondness.

As he passed, she wondered why she had thought herself in love with him and considered marriage to him at one time. Her father Clay treated her like his father treated his mother. The men in her family were indulgent with their women. "Come to think of it," she thought, "Judah is a lot like my father *and* grandfather."

The thought of Judah made her wonder just where he was at present, and whether Ben was with him. Foolish woman that she was, she made it plain that she didn't want to hear from him when she left *The Crossing* that final day.

And to Marnie's distress, Judah honored her request.

Did Judah think of her? She had not even brought a picture of him with her. Did he take one of her with him when he left *The Crossing*? Had she turned her son against her, too? He had left in July but there had been no word from him since his departure.

She heaved a deep sigh, and turned her attention back to the meeting.

Clay Spencer locked the doors and was headed for bed.

"Pa?"

He turned to look at her. "What is it, Marnie?"

"I—I just wanted to know what the meeting was about, that's all."

"Now, miss. If I wanted you to know, I would have invited you into the office."

She opened her mouth to argue, but Clay dismissed her with a chuck under the chin. "You don't need to worry your pretty head about such things." He leaned his cheek toward her. "I'm going to bed now. Now, give me a kiss, daughter."

Marnie leaned in to kiss his cheek, and then as a preoccupied look passed over his face, Clay hurried for his bedroom.

She was able to wangle most things out of her father, but it was apparent that she would get no information about the meeting. Somber lot, the men were, when they filed out the door, and she knew instinctively that something was about to happen. Just what, she did not know, but she was sure that it wouldn't be long before she found out.

CHAPTER FOURTEEN

IT WAS A TRYING TIME in Clinton County for anyone to stay out of the conflict. Though Kentucky had in a sense struck hands with both the North and South, it was not able to stay neutral for long. There were those on both sides who were adamant that men should choose one side or the other, and Clay Spencer was among those who were most vocal for the Union. The favorite topic when men met was war, and Confederate activity across the border was cause for alarm.

In the days to come, men were coming and going from Clay Spencer's ranch. Cloaked with secrecy, they made no pretense that their business there was anything but of utmost importance.

Try as she would, Marnie could elicit no information from her father and it began to wear thin. Seth was around more than usual, and even he was closed-mouthed.

"Mae," asked Marnie, "do you know what is going on…all Pa's friends coming and going and all?"

She shrugged her shoulders. "No, Marnie, I sure don't. It seems mighty peculiar to me, all this activity going on of a sudden. Usually, your father is transparent as spring water, but, I'll tell you, I've never seen him so secretive. If you ask me, it spells nothing but trouble…surely, nothing but trouble."

Mae made a clucking noise. "I'd be mighty careful what I do, if I were you. That Harmon family down the road are Southern sympathizers, and if something is about to happen, you ought to think about staying away from there."

Mae shook her head. "I know you've been looking in on Bessie Harmon, her having a baby and all, and you've been doctorin' others too, but you'd better watch your step. Take my word, something's about to blow wide open in this county."

Marnie was distraught. How could she refuse help if the residents of the county called for her? That was something she felt she could not do. And what would her father say? This may be one time that he would listen to Seth McCord concerning her "traipsings about", as Seth so often called it. She wished Judah was with her so that she could talk to him about the matter. He wouldn't refuse, that she was sure of.

Finally, one early evening in September, her father, armed as though he were going to the battle front, his pockets sagging heavy with ammunition, left the house in the long twilight. In his eyes she could read a recklessness that she had often seen in the eyes of his twin brother, Cole Spencer. Although Cole was the manager of *Stone Valley Springs Hotel*, he was always ready at the spur of the moment for devilment of one sort or another.

Something was wrong. Something was wrong with her father, Seth, and the men they consorted with, something wrong with the whole county! She could sense it and yet could not define exactly what it was she was feeling. These men meeting as they had been were acting unusual. They were secretive, exhilarated. They were up to no good, she was sure of that. Yet, not one opened their mouth to her.

Clay was headed for the barn and after a few minutes she followed him there. He exited the building leading his horse into the corral.

"Where are you going, Pa," she questioned, worry turning to insistence in her voice, "with night coming on?"

All the answer she got was a glimpse of Clay's glittering dark eyes, the dangers of the evening affecting him like an intoxicant, and a springy stride in his steps. Marnie followed him as he passed through the gate and for one swift moment a flash of setting sunlight shone on the rifle barrel as he shoved it into the scabbard.

Mounting his horse, he whipped off his hat with a sweeping gesture and spoke loudly into the coming night as though he were a knight in shining armor, "I shall return, daughter," and with that said, settled the hat back on his head, and jerked the reins and turned, riding off, jumping a rail fence, hooves thundering down the drive.

Marnie stared after him, heart swelling with something she couldn't define if she'd had the presence of mind to think of it. Hardly aware that she was moving, she absently meandered around, eventually ending in the apple orchard, wondering passionately what was going on in Albany for she had caught snatches of the name of their county seat a couple of times in their murmurings. Just what Albany had to do with their schemes, she did not know. As if the war talk wasn't bad enough already!

Clay's outspokenness would be his undoing, she prophetically thought, absently plucking a leaf from a loaded apple tree. The apples were ready for picking, but that fact escaped her attention for the present as the concern for her father shrouded all other thoughts. She had never known him to be anything but a hard working family man, but this war had changed him…and not for the better! It was as though the war had given him a new purpose in life and one that was not altogether becoming in her opinion. He was not alone in his fanaticism though, for everyone in the county seemed possessed with a frenzied patriotism she did not possess. And this devotion was dividing the county in a way she had never seen while growing up here. Neighbor against neighbor. Brother against brother.

Talk was escalating out of control. Not that she had always had an understanding of men, for on more than one occasion she observed when men had growled and heckled about, in a matter of minutes they acted like best friends. It was all very bewildering, indeed.

But this went beyond that kind of interaction, she sensed. They had not yet taken up arms against one another. However…why did Pa leave here with so much ammunition? she asked herself.

And now, fear of unknown things, seized her and spurred her into action. As twilight was fading, Marnie suddenly made a decision. It didn't matter that it would soon be night. She would ride to Albany in the dark, unafraid, to see firsthand what mischief had occurred at the hands of these men. To think that Clay and Seth would take her to task did not enter into her mind, and it would not have mattered to her if they had.

Her heart racing, she ran quickly to the barn for her horse. So feverishly was her thinking, that her fingers felt like all thumbs trying to saddle her horse. She led her gray out of the corral and stepped into the saddle, intending to ride to the house and inform Mae of her decision. She had not made it to the front door when Mae and Judith descended the porch steps.

"Just where," demanded Mae, hands on her hips, "do you think you're going, missy?"

"I'm riding to Albany. Don't wait up for me," she said hurriedly.

"Oh, no, ma'am, you don't! Not in this dark of night, you're not." Mae warned and took a step forward. "It's no telling what might befall you out there riding all by yourself."

"Oh, yes, I am!" she argued determinedly. Looking at her daughter, she said, "Take care of Judith." And with that, she wheeled her horse and headed for Albany.

Mae shook her head. "Um, um, um. Bull-headed that child is and has always been," declared Maè as Marnie rode off. "Mark my word," she continued as she turned to Judith, "that brashness is going to get your mother in trouble someday!"

And she continued her grumbling as she climbed the steps and passed through the door.

Judith, however, watched as her mother disappeared out of sight. She felt secure with her mother. In the absence of her father, Judith was confident no harm would come to her, for who would surely harm a child of Marnie Cross?

As far back as she could remember, her mother had always had a quality of strength about her, kept in check, of course, by her father Judah. Since the war had started and her father was gone, that strength became more predominant, but her mother did not smile as much anymore and it worried her at times.

Though she didn't say so, those times of concern were when her mother took her medicine chest and started out alone to tend to someone sick. Seth McCord was very vocal about it, and in her silence, Judith agreed. However, these were different times, she reasoned, and who was she to take her mother to task?

Something else lay heavy on Judith's heart and she had intended talking to her mother about it. She had received a letter. Her beau, Zane Banyon, at *The Crossing* had joined the Union cavalry. Her mother would understand how she felt for she worried about Zane even as her mother was disquiet about her father Judah.

More than that, though, how would she feel about Zane turning over the management of the property to Wade Caulder. It's not that her mother had anything against Wade, but she was adamant about responsibility, and Wade was remiss when it came to dependability. No…she decided, it would not do to tell her mother the news as it would add to the worries she already had.

With a heavy sigh, Judith turned and climbed the steps to the porch. Telling Mae would not be the same, but it would have to do for now.

CHAPTER FIFTEEN

IT WAS DARK, yet a night when the moon and stars were brilliant when Marnie rode into Albany, and found the town was a beehive of activity. Riding slowly, she saw a woman watching down the street from the second floor. A door slammed somewhere, voices were buzzing with excitement, and horses standing three legged and mules were tethered to the hitching rails. A great crowd was gathered at the courthouse and she pulled up her horse and watched, studying the assembly.

Scanning their faces in the light of the street lanterns, she found hard indifference there, or hatred. In no face did she see warmth or a friendly feeling. She frowned thoughtfully. Trouble was afoot, of that she had no doubt. Just what it was, she was determined to find out. There were no ladies in the crowd, with the exception of a few on the boardwalk that had been pressed out of curiosity to come. She sat astride her horse, debating whether to dismount and gather the courage to walk into the courthouse to find out what had caused such an assembly.

To the side of her a man's voice sounded. "Well..." he said in evident surprise, "good evening, Miss Cross." She turned and glanced down at the man.

It was Lee Cannon and smiling over clenched white teeth that gripped his cigar, he took off his hat to her, and the smile that curled his lips had no warmth. “I’m surprised to see you in town tonight with all this going on.”

Lee Cannon was a heavy-set man, a stubble of graying beard covering his jowls. The grizzled beard made him seem older than he really was. She did not know him very well, except for the fact he was one of the men that met her father at the ranch.

“Pray, tell, Mr. Cannon,” she asked dryly. “Exactly what *is* going on?”

“Haven’t you heard?” he asked as he replaced his hat.

“Heard what?”

“Well, ma’am,” he said, sticking his chest out in an act of importance, “we’ve rounded up all the Confederate sympathizers in this county and slapped them in jail, we did, and all without firing a single shot. Put ‘em right where they belong!” he said gleefully.

That was what they had been plotting! A few men she had known in the past were always hinting at how silly women were, but they couldn’t have been any sillier in this mindless act of aggression. They were still at peace in this part of Kentucky and it was as though they were inviting, nay, rather, daring war to engage in Clinton County. For a swift instant there went through her mind a scene of Confederates crossing the border into Clinton County. They would be all right for they had their secret valley with their stock intact. But what of her neighbors? What of the old? What of the young wives and children? Who would look after them now that they were bereft of male protection?

Marnie was hard pressed to speak civilly to Lee Cannon. “Oh, yes, I do see,” she said stiffly, and nodded at the rifle in his hand. ”And the sheriff doesn’t object?”

He smiled as if he’d won first prize at a turkey shoot. “Wouldn’t do much good,” he cackled. “All this scuttlebutt we’ve been hearing about, we thought it about time to nip it in the bud.”

Pompous fool! she thought, and then she hastily remembered the Bible saying not to call anyone a fool. “But I can’t help it,” she thought with a sharp shake of her head. "They're acting like a passel of them! Foolish, they all are!"

"Who is 'we', if I may ask?" she asked, sarcasm just below the surface.

"Why, ma'am," he said, his eyes opened wide with surprise, "I thought you knew all about that. Your own Pa is one of the leaders…and a right good leader, he is, if I say so myself."

And to think there wasn't enough to worry about!

"Just why would I know that, Mr. Cannon?"

"Well…" he said thoughtfully, "maybe you wouldn't at that.

"So…you've taken matters into your own hands," she stated coolly, her eyes faintly ironic. "You're doing nothing but stirring up trouble!"

The smile slowly slipped from his face. He took the cigar out of his mouth, and leaning over, spat onto the grass. "Ma'am, this is war, it is," he replied, arrogance in his voice. "Things are different now. The sheriff can't take care of things. Our Home Guard are keeping the peace for our folks," and promptly placed the cigar back in his teeth.

She smiled a slow smile. "If you can help me understand, Mr. Cannon, can you tell me has there been some trouble recently? Anyone hurt or killed?"

He took the cigar from between his teeth again in thought. "Well…as a matter of fact, no, not in any sense of the word, in this county, that is. But it's been brewing so we're just heading it off, so to speak."

"Heading it off," she repeated. "I see. Is that what you call it?" she stated skeptically.

A questioning look came on his face. "I'm afraid I don't know exactly what you're getting at, ma'am."

She recovered herself and said, "I'm not getting at anything, Mr. Cannon. Tell me…is my father among that crowd?"

"Yes, he is. In fact, he's been pretty much at the head of all this tonight. Proud to say I know him, I am."

She started to answer when she saw Seth making his way through the swarm of men, giving her an inscrutable look.

Reaching them, he nodded to Lee, “Cannon.”

“Seth. Fine job we did, didn’t we?”

Seth merely dismissed him with a look and turned to Marnie. Lee Cannon, understanding the look, moved back toward the crowd.

Seth looked up at her, his eyes frank and cool with barely tamped-down fury.

“I suppose it’s useless to ask what you’re doing here,” he said.

“I’ve come about Pa. Tell me, where is he?”

He nodded toward the courthouse. “In there.”

She started to dismount, but as he laid a hand on the horse’s mane, she stopped and settled back down again in the saddle.

“I don’t think it’s a good idea for you to go in there just now,” he advised.

“I think,” she chided, anger rising to the forefront, “you ran out of good ideas a long time ago, Seth McCord.”

Seth dropped his hand, and then ran it over the back of his neck in frustration.

“I’m not going to argue with you, Marnie. If you’ll wait a few minutes, I’ll get my horse and see you back home.”

“I’m not going home without Pa.”

“You might want to think about that. I don’t believe he’s ready to leave *or* in the mood.”

“Go get him! If you won’t, then I’ll get him myself,” she said adamantly, as she prepared to throw a leg over the horse to dismount.

Seth threw up a hand, capitulating. “All right. Hold on,” he said. “I’ll go see what I can do.”

As Marnie waited, she watched the men cavorting in triumph. She struggled to stay calm, sensing they were being drawn into a conflict they’d best stay clear of. But who was she that they would listen to? She felt like John the Baptist in the Bible.

A voice crying in the wilderness.

It wasn't long until Seth reappeared, Clay following behind. Coming through the crowd, Clay was practically crowing, his face florid with excitement as men offered their congratulations to him.

Dismounting and leading her horse, Marnie drew away from the crowd as Clay and Seth approached and they joined her under a grove of trees near the center of town.

"What were you thinking of," she turned suddenly and asked Clay, as the noise of the Home Guard continued, "rounding all those men up like that and bringing them to jail?" Her voice was not pleasant. She did not feel pleasant.

Seth's face thinned down. "Marnie, now you keep out of this," Seth interrupted as Clay began to open his mouth to answer. "This is man's business!"

The fools—all of them! This whole thing had gotten out of hand! For the first time since she could ever remember, Marnie wanted to shake Seth McCord. She wanted it so that the tears in her eyes were there as much from anger as much from sorrow. Wanted it so strong it shook her like the ague. She wanted it so that her hands shook and her voice trembled.

"Man's business?" she said and burst into a laugh that was cutting with contempt.

"Since when is it *man's* business, unsettling everything?" she challenged. "Don't you think the women and children will suffer because of this? How dare you take matters into your own hands!"

"Now, Marnie," Seth answered, fury flickering across his face, "we're just trying to *protect* the women and children."

"Protect! Protect? Is that what you call it? No, you're not!" she replied. "You're just stirring things up, making things worse than they already are!"

She snorted, her mouth pursing scornfully. "Are you coming home?" she asked her father.

"I—I—" Clay stammered weakly, his hands spread wide open in defense.

“He can’t tonight,” Seth answered firmly. “We have to guard the prisoners.”

Clay spoke with far more calm than he was feeling. “Marnie, dear, please leave this to us. I’m sure everything will turn out all right. After all, the enemy is entrenched in our very midst. I promise…I’ll come home shortly.”

Marnie had come so hurriedly that she forgot to bring a jacket. It was turning cool at night and she shivered, not so much from the night air, but what she imagined what might come of their action. Union troops from North of the Cumberland River were not here to protect the citizens of the county and they were left on their own. Why could they not understand that it would be better to try to live in peace with their neighbors that were for the Confederacy? Friends they had been for years. Friends that now were considered enemies.

Her eyes were wide, her face white as she turned first to Clay and then Seth, her lips forming an unspoken protest. For an instant they stared at each other, and when her anger flared in impotency, she turned on her heel and stepped into the saddle, and with a jerk of the reins, turned, and clapping her heels against the animal’s sides, rode quickly away out of town.

Clay watched her retreating back. Could it be that Marnie saw a different side to this? Had he and the others been too hasty in their actions? Would something untoward, indeed, come from all this?

“I think you were a bit too hard on her,” Clay softly chided Seth.

“And I think you’re too soft on her, Clay,” Seth retorted. “You just wait, we’ll have this thing wrapped up before you know it,” he said boastfully.

Seth’s words rang hollow in his ears and he stared gloomily at Marnie until the darkness swallowed her up.

“Maybe,” Clay answered thoughtfully, removing his hat and scratching his head. “But you’ve got to admit, Seth. Marnie *did* make a valid point.”

CHAPTER SIXTEEN

SHE'D HARDLY returned home and caught her breath when a knock sounded on the door. She opened it and there stood Cary Harmon, sister-in-law of Bessie Harmon.

"Bessie said for you to come," said Cary.

"It's her time?" asked Marnie.

Cary shook her head. "Yes."

Marnie glanced at the sky. It was beginning to paint the landscape with sepia light. It would rain today. She could smell it in the air.

"I'll be right with you," she said, leaving the door open, and turned to get her medical bag.

Riding along with Cary Harmon, Marnie was glad to have a distraction from last night's fiasco. Of course, none of the small band of men involved would call it that. It was more like retribution from their point of view. To her, it was a wonder they did not take out an advertisement in the newspaper proclaiming their victory. How she hated the war!

Giving a small gasp, it suddenly dawned on her that she was riding toward a house of Confederate sympathizers. Was Bessie's husband, Stephen among those that were taken prisoner last night? If so, why would they send for her knowing that Judah and Benjamin served in Federal forces? And how could she justify what her own father had done to his neighbors?

Her fears subsided a bit when Cary gave no indication that such a thing had occurred, but then she thought of her own family and their secret of the valley where the livestock was kept. Although the county was sorely divided, she sensed others were keeping their own secrets as well. Survival was on the minds of everyone.

And survival would be on the mind of Bessie Harmon. For Confederate or Union, any woman in labor would accept help from anyone who could help deliver her child safely.

Arriving at the small cabin and walking through the door, her first thought was about Stephen. Even as Cary led her to the small bedroom, her eyes darted around for a glimpse of him, but without success.

The room was shuttered against the clouded day. Bessie laid on the bed, a girl with long brown hair, and soft brown eyes which were a little anxious at the sight of Marnie. She was sixteen years old, Stephen eighteen. He had not joined the military and never indicated any intention of doing so. His father and brothers had enlisted with the Confederacy after Tennessee had seceded. The Harmon family was a large clan in Clinton County with relatives in Tennessee, and to offend one Harmon would offend all.

After a preliminary examination, she asked, "When did your pains begin, Bessie?"

"Last night," she answered.

"And you didn't send for me?"

"I did, but you weren't home."

Marnie felt a dart go through her at that. No, she wasn't home, and all her running to town didn't accomplish anything at all.

"Well," she said, forcing hopefulness in her tone, "first babies usually take longer. How have you been feeling?"

Bessie's eyes were wide with soft urgency. "Not too well, Marnie. I seem to be so tired all the time."

Marnie scrutinized closer the head lying on the pillow, hair fanned out around her. Bessie's face was a little pale, but it was always pale. The youngest of a large family, she was also the smallest and had seemed very delicate. Marnie began to worry that this birth might not be as easy as most that she and Judah had attended to.

"That's normal," she said optimistically, instead.

Her pains were very hard and long and Marnie knew it wouldn't be long before the baby came. To distract Bessie after a contraction, she asked, "By the way, where's Stephen? I thought he'd be here with you."

Bessie quickly dropped her eyes, prompting an uneasy feeling in Marnie. "He—he had to go someplace this morning. I'm not sure just where, but I hope he'll be back before the baby's born."

"This morning," she had said. So Stephen was not one of the men taken in the raid last night. Had he some knowledge about what was happening last night and escaped? If so, where could he be then? In hiding?

Hour after hour passed, and as the afternoon wore on, Bessie, her gown wet with perspiration, twisted endlessly, to one side, to the other, to left, to right and back again. Moaning and sometimes screaming, something was wrong. Marnie examined her again. Breech birth! And she had no forceps!

Marnie had attended a few such births with Judah. He had actually performed surgery, lifting the baby out of the womb, but she wasn't an expert surgeon! Bessie could die, and if she tried to operate she might kill her anyway!

Judah! I need you! Bessie needs you! Oh, God, please help me deliver this baby!

It was all over. The small baby boy was receiving his first bath at the hands of Cary. It was no small wonder that Bessie was not dead and was sleeping after what she had been through. Only the grace of God intervened, for Marnie had seen several women die in childbirth in normal deliveries.

Twilight was descending like a curtain over a day that would remain acutely in her memory, and Marnie, in wonderment that it was the end of the day, crossed the porch slowly, like an old woman, sat on the step of the front porch, breathing in the fresh air after the stuffiness of the cabin. Weary, she leaned her head against the post of the porch, pushed back her hair that had come undone, and unbuttoned her basque halfway down her bosom. She wanted to thank God for his intervention, but felt too tired to do anything but sleep.

She had developed a tension headache which now had dulled to a consistent throb, and she pressed her fingers to her aching temples. There was movement by Cary in the cabin, and perhaps she should help, but Marnie was in no mood to be with people just now.

Her mind was a vacuity. She succumbed to nothingness, did not want to think of this day or anything. Not war, politics, nothing! She had gone without sleep for two days and a night and slowly, laboriously stretched out on the porch, heedless of what anyone would say, intending spending the night right where she was. It was so quiet that she heard the sound of her own breathing, and then there were sounds of hoof beats coming up the road.

If that was Stephen Harmon, then it was high time he showed up! She wanted to take him to task, but felt too tired. Seemed like she wanted to take everyone to task lately!

From the shadow of the porch, she wearily turned her head to the side and, instead of Stephen, saw both Clay and Seth approaching warily.

They reined their horses in when they saw her lying there.

"Marnie!" Clay called, terror in his voice.

She merely stared and didn't answer.

A quick gallop of the horses brought them to the porch and both men were off their animals before coming to a complete stop.

"Marnie, girl! Are you alright?" asked Clay, gathering her in his arms while Seth cautiously surveyed the cabin for any movement about.

"I'm fine, Pa." She struggled to sit up. "Bessie had her baby a while ago."

"I thought when I saw you lying there, that you were dead."

She managed a slight smile. "I feel pretty close to it. I'm exhausted."

"Is Stephen Harmon about?" asked Seth without apparent thought for anything else.

Marnie glared at him. She didn't want to think of last night and what the nightriders had done. She wanted to say, 'Thank you for asking about my health' in a spiteful manner, but said instead, "I haven't seen him."

Seth opened his mouth again, but she interrupted and said, "Bessie doesn't know where he is either, if that's what you are about to ask."

"He wasn't here last night," Seth stated accusingly. "I rode by here."

"I don't know anything about that, but I don't think it's wise to speak of it on the man's own front porch," she ventured a little acidly.

"You're right, Marnie," Clay said, taken down a peg, a pained expression on his face. He helped her up. "Let's get her home, Seth.

She was so tired…had wanted to go straight to bed once arriving home from Bessie Harmon's, but Mae wouldn't hear of it.

"Marnie, you are going to eat some supper before you go to bed," Mae said, her brow furrowed with indignation, casting a furtive look at Clay. "You've been over there taking care of Confederates, wearing yourself out, and it's time you took care of yourself."

Clay chanced a look at Mae. She had always aired her views when Marnie traversed the county tending the sick before she was married. But for all her arguments, Clay had turned a deaf ear. And he turned one now, as always.

Barely had they sat down to supper, when an urgent knock sounded at the door. Before Clay could reach it, another knock sounded, urgent and louder this time.

He opened the door and Theron Bales pushed his way past him.

"Wha—?"

As Theron stepped inside, he saw that Clay had a pistol in his hand. He stared at it and then glanced up to see Clay's eyes.

"You never know who's going to come through a door," Clay said, shrugging his shoulders. He placed the pistol down on a small table, and then turned to face Theron.

Theron recovered from his initial shock and stated emphatically, "Clay!"

"What is it, Theron?" Clay asked.

Theron place his hand on Clay's arm. "Clay, you've got to come back to town."

"Trouble?" he asked as his hand automatically moved toward the pistol again.

"Trouble!" he exclaimed. "I'd say! A courier got through to Confederate Captain Bledsoe about the raid. We've got word that he's coming across the state line from Jamestown, Tennessee with a company of men to set free the rebel sympathizers. It's not to be borne! Not in Clinton County. Those Tennessee rebels have no business here!"

Clay stood immobile for a few seconds, digesting the news Theron brought.

"Move, man!" Theron prodded. "They're coming. We've got a fight on our hands!"

Clay Spencer sprang into action, and retrieving his rifle and ammunition raced with Theron to the courthouse.

At Clay's leave-taking, Marnie wanted to go with him, but the wild look on his face forbade her from asking. After he had gone, she was restless, had gone to her bedroom to pray. But unable to drop to her knees, she walked the floor and merely repeated anxiously, "God, help him…God help him."

In spite of her fatigue, it was almost midnight before Marnie retired to bed. During most of that time she had tried to plan some course of action for the morrow. She was no soldier, was not proficient in marksmanship of weapons, but if her father were to be taken prisoner by Bledsoe, she would not hesitate to go after him. Just what she would do, she did not know, but she would not sit idle.

Somewhere along the tangled trail of her thoughts she dropped off and slept, and while she slept, the fight started in Albany. It was a brief skirmish at the courthouse, the few Home Guard present retreated quickly, outnumbered by Bledsoe's company. How the Confederate sympathizers would now laugh! The former bluster of their captors now dissolved into fear!

Making off with Home Guards' 30 odd muskets and 3,000 rounds of ammunition, Bledsoe's company returned across the county line.

Doing what Home Guard thought was right, this one act by the Unionists in the county brought more trouble than anything that had occurred so far.

Peace, as they had known it, was over for Clinton County.

CHAPTER SEVENTEEN

THROUGHOUT THE END of the year 1861, Clinton County residents experienced occupation of both Union and Confederate forces alternately.

After the arrest of Confederate allies and the liberation of the captured by Captain Bledsoe, Lieutenant Morrison's company was ordered from Camp Dick Robinson to Albany. Colonel William Hoskins returned with his infantry to Albany the end of September. He arrived amid wild rumors that rebel forces menacing Clinton County numbered one thousand and was expected to return at any time.

In response, Hoskins had dispatched messengers calling upon the Home Guards of Casey and Adair Counties to assist him in defending Albany.

For the Union supporters, this temporary influx of Federal forces buoyed up the spirits of the Union residents and they felt safer going abroad in the county.

When Marnie heard the Adair County Home Guard was in town, she wasted no time in convincing her father to take her to Albany! Adair County was the place of her estate *The Crossing*, and she longed for any news of how it was faring.

The night before had been wet with rain, but when Marnie and Clay rode into Albany the warm sun was at work, drying the streets of mud. Pickets were posted along the roads and guards were posted all over town, and there was a jubilant atmosphere about the town that uplifted her. As they made their way through the mudholes of the main street, Marnie noted the sidewalks were crowded with residents from the county looking to resupply from the stores, some of what Duke Morgan and his men had stolen from them.

Clay stopped and conversed with a few of the men. Talk turned to war. Talk always turned to war now. Any conversation on a particular topic inevitably led to war, and as firmly as Marnie changed the subject, it always led back to war. War weddings, who had left to join and where, accompanied with pride for those who had left, and most recently, the raidings of Duke Morgan's small band upon their homes.

Driving to the north end of town where the troops and Home Guard units were bivouacked, the town was humming like a beehive. Two thousand men with artillery were fortifying the place. Marnie was shocked at the sight of so many soldiers. Was it truly that serious of a state Clinton County was in, and furthermore, how did they feed so many men?

With Marnie at his heels, Clay worked his way through the mass of soldiers, and by the direction of a captain, located the Adair County Home Guard. There they spotted his brother Cole at a washtub, washing a few clothes.

"Cole," Clay shouted. "Cole Spencer."

Marnie followed his gaze, and saw a familiar sight. There stood her Uncle Cole, the spitting image of his brother Clay, except for the beginning of a dark beard that now sported his face.

Cole turned, his hands covered in white suds. Wiping his hands down his pants, he made his way to where Clay and Marnie were standing and a smile of pleasure spread over his face.

"Cole Spencer," said Marnie laughingly, "I never thought I'd see the day when you would be slaving over a tub of suds."

He saluted her and grinned, and the smile was the smile of his twin brother Clay. "All in the line of duty, ma'am. All in the line of duty. Just because I've come to fight doesn't mean I have to do it in dirty clothes," he jokingly said.

"Dear Cole," she thought affectionately, "he saw a joke in everything if he thought there was any merit to it."

"I had hoped to see you, Clay," he, turning sober, addressed his brother. "We just got in this morning, and I assume you know firsthand the situation here."

Clay and Cole spoke of the war a few moments and then Marnie interrupted. She had a hundred questions on her mind, and before she left, she wanted answers that had been unrequited thus far.

"Please, Pa," she pleaded, laying a hand on his arm. "Cole, have you heard from Judah or Benjamin?"

"Benjamin enlisted?" Cole said, surprised.

"Yes, in August. He was going to Camp Dick Robinson to be with Judah."

"No, Marnie, I sure haven't," answered Cole, his face serious.

"I wouldn't worry so much, if I were you," he said, with a laugh. "Judah will be patching the men up, and it could be Benjamin will help him."

His laughter failed to allay her fears. When there were no soldiers about in the county of either side, war seemed distant to her with the exception of the safety of her two men with Wolford's Cavalry. But looking about her now, she realized this was just an inkling of what was to come. It was daunting, to say the least. Truly, what were they to face? Was she brave enough, strong enough to come through?

"What of the hotel, Cole?" she asked, bringing her mind back to the present. "What's happening there?"

He scratched his head and said, "Well, not a whole lot right now. Everything's in an uproar with so many enlisting. So many folks have gone home and not many are making reservations to stay."

He laughed. "Would you believe it? Mother and Pa are there right now taking care of things. I didn't think there was anything that could drag Mother away from North Star."

Marnie was stunned. Grandfather Judge Sam Spencer and Grandmother Rachel at Stone Valley Springs Resort?

"But, Uncle Cole!" she exclaimed as Clay uttered something unintelligible. "They must be well in their eighties!"

"Early nineties," he corrected. "And Pa's having the time of his life, threatening to join the Home Guard, he is, but you know Mother. She keeps talking about getting crops in, and is in a passion to leave the hotel to get back to North Star. I don't know how she's going to harvest much though. There's not many hands left with the war going on. She's hired some schoolboys to work the place, but they can't do the job that men can."

He laughed again. "She'll ride herd on them, though, even if she has to hobble on a cane to do it."

"Pa…in the Home Guard?" Clay marveled, and pictured his elderly father in a rifle pit in knee-deep mud somewhere in battle with the rebel army.

"Oh," Cole waved a hand at the air at the look on Clay's face, "I wouldn't worry about it. That will never happen. Mother absolutely forbids it, and you know Pa does pretty much what Mother says."

A knife-like pain went through Marnie. How often she had rehearsed in her mind the fact that Judah left her. In a way, she was jealous of Grandmother Rachel and the sway she held over her husband. It was not that Grandmother was overbearing, but Judge Sam seemed so smitten with her, even after nearly sixty-five years of marriage. She had even been told that he could have had been a prominent figure in the Kentucky Legislature years ago, but chose to stay in Adair County with his wife. Not that he hadn't been busy in Adair County all these years…he had. Serving as judge and minister, he had influenced the county for good.

Judah was different, she had to admit. He never let her influence him in decisions he felt was right. So reserved at times, she was never able to completely break down his detachment, even in lovemaking. His kisses, though loving, were never with abandoned passion, and at times she thought that was just the way of a man…until she would see her grandmother and grandfather together, their way of touching, and fond regard on their faces when looking at one another.

"Oh, by the way," Cole said offhandedly, interrupting her thoughts, "Zane Banyon has joined the cavalry. But I suppose Judith has told you."

She was struck dumb for a moment. *Zane?* In the army? And he didn't even write to let her know? A bit of irritation at his dereliction in duties riddled her.

Cole intimated Judith knew? How would Judith have known? Zane was foreman of *The Crossing* while Judah was home. Now that Zane had gone, who has taken his place? This, she asked Cole.

"Zane told me that Wade Caulder is overseeing things now," and seeing the disparaging look on her face, proffered, "and you're mighty lucky to have him since so many men have joined up."

Wade Caulder? She supposed she needed to count herself lucky as he said, but he was not the quality of foreman that Zane Banyon was. Zane had, for a lack of a better word, flash, and had a certain flamboyance about him that bordered on carelessness. He was like a knight in shining armor, a man without reserve and he could charm the wings off of bees. To her apprehension, he had certainly swept Judith off her feet. She supposed she should not have been surprised at the news for Zane was impetuous at times, and only Judah alone had kept him in line.

But Wade? He never had much to say, never displayed any sparkle, and was often silent. But he did his work patiently and competently. She finally decided that she was grateful that Wade was as steady as he was. He would take care of things at home…that she was sure of.

It was a different time, for sure, and she hoped the war would not last too long. For that was what the men were saying. 'No, sir!' they declared. 'The Confederates would not win over the Union.'

The threat of Confederate soldiers was no longer on the lips or faces of men and women…for the time being, at least.

CHAPTER EIGHTEEN

THE INVASION of Clinton County by the Confederates of Tennessee failed to materialize. The Home Guards of Casey and Adair Counties, tired of waiting for an attack from the enemy, returned home. Toward the end of October Federal Forces retired back north of the Cumberland River, about forty miles from Albany and the Confederates occupied the county once again, passing through and made a short stay at Albany and driving off horses, cattle, and hogs.

A storm had blown up and the woods were deep in chestnuts, acorns, and hickory nuts. Mae suggested gathering the nuts to store for winter, and Marnie and Judith set about gathering them. In four days' time they had collected so many they needed the wagon to haul them home. Back at the house the three of them began the tedious process of taking the hulls off before storing them for winter. Mae recommended some of the acorns be parched for coffee and grind the rest into flour in the event coffee and flour become scarce during the war.

Marnie had never had acorn coffee in her life, not even while growing up and before marriage, and wondered just how it tasted. Others had in Clinton County, but her father loved coffee and had always insisted on real coffee beans. She became tickled thinking of the look on her father's face as he tasted acorn coffee.

Having been called to the Bales cabin some distance away, Marnie packed a small kettle of victuals and her medicine bag and left. Clay was at the valley and she had not seen Seth for several days.

The trees were showing the slightest hint of turning into their fall colors, and the sunlight was streaking through them.

Not once did she think of war trouble as she rode. Mae had said this morning the last of the apples needed to be picked and dried, reserving some for applesauce, and the rest of the corn should be harvested as fodder for the livestock. Wood needed to be chopped for the winter and the rest of the nuts dried. So many things to do before the hard chill of winter set in. The woods seemed peaceable, and she felt peaceful as she had not for several months.

Her heart and her mind were wandering from chore to chore, and she barely heard the tramping of horses until they were upon her.

Pulling up, she turned and saw Duke Morgan with his small band of men, and as they drew rein, the men seemed as mettlesome and dangerous as the high spirited horses they rode. Duke sat astride a white stallion and Marnie took note they were all riding quality animals. "Wonder who they stole them from?" she thought.

"Marnie!" Duke exclaimed, shifting his seat in the saddle, his surprise an obvious pretense. "You're riding out here alone?"

Though she did not know or remember most of the men that were riding with him, one alone stood out. She had seen him in Albany with Duke. Bob Witter was his name, and he was known to be wild and reckless as well as haughty and insulting. He had gambled away the property his father left him after he died and he was a known drunkard. Although she had known his name and his deeds for several years now through her father, she had never seen him at close range as at the present. His eyes burned curiously as they stared at her, the eyes of a man who was not mentally normal.

Marnie looked coolly at Bob Witter before answering. Inwardly, she was far from cool, for she could see Bob would turn on her at the least provocation. She realized it with an intuition that warned her that the man was dangerous.

"Duke Morgan," she said quietly, turning her eyes back to him, "everyone knows I ride alone…including you," she retorted, chafing at his mock surprise.

The veracity of her tone amused him, for he did indeed know that. In fact, he knew most of what went on in the county.

"Don't you know," he admonished, "it's quite dangerous for you to be out by yourself?" She had heard that so many times she wanted to scream.

Marnie pushed out her lips in mute indignation at being told how to conduct her own business, and then she said with a faint shadowing of contempt, "Who am I to be afraid of, Duke…you?" Turning to look at Bob Witter, "Or them?"

Something changed in Bob Witter's eyes, and into his face came an indication that she was marked for death.

Duke was taken aback at her bravado and the rest of his men chuckled at her brazen reply. Duke's lips did not smile but suddenly his eyes twinkled. She had gumption, he had to give her that much. She had always had a way about her…her way. But with the few bands of guerrillas from Tennessee moving about, he suddenly worried. They did not know her as he did, did not love her as he once did…and still did to a degree.

"There's danger out here," he argued logically. He nearly called her 'honey' but caught himself in time. "You don't know what you're getting yourself into."

"That's what everyone tells me," she said a little sharply. She sighed and her voice became softer. "My only danger, Duke, is not getting in time to the folks that need my help."

His brows knit together in contemplation and he clucked his tongue against his teeth in thought.

"Your father is on the wrong side of this war, Marnie, as well as Judah and your son. And because of their views, I don't think it's a good idea for you to be out and about."

Marnie stared at him for she didn't know if the threat was coming from him and his band or some of the other guerrillas that ventured in the area from time to time.

She took a deep breath and drew from a deep well of patience.

"Listen, Duke," she said with resignation, but she smiled when she spoke. "I really don't care whose side anybody is on, whether it's you or Pa, or my family. I've been against this war from the beginning and don't hold with either side, and my only concern is for the sick. Now if you think it's necessary to try to stop me, go ahead and shoot me!" she dared him. "But I'll tell you right now, I will serve as doctor to anyone, whether they are Union or Confederate.

"You didn't like what I said, did you? Perhaps I should have said something nice or patriotic like everyone else! I've got my work to do, and frankly, that's all I really care about at the moment."

She felt a sense of relief to finally completely speak her mind. To no one had she intimated that she was for or against either side. She just wanted peace and her men back home.

He studied her as she spoke, his eyes on her face. In all reality, what Duke was thinking was that he admired her spirit. What a woman she would be, if she declared herself for the Confederacy! He had been in love with her at one time, and though her confidence in herself had bothered him at times, that same confidence won him over now.

She felt a bit scattered sitting astride her horse so near him and wondered if she looked as scattered as she felt.

"You need have no fear of us, Marnie," he promised quietly. "Go about your business, as usual. You have my word. You won't be harmed. I'll spread the word to—I'll spread the word that you are not to be touched."

He then gave orders to his men that if she were injured by any one of them, he would personally kill him, and he specifically directed his eyes at Bob Witter as he said it, even though he was his friend. Bob Witter didn't take it too kindly, but he knew what Duke

Morgan was capable of. What Duke said is what Duke meant, and though they were friends, it would not do to cross him.

"By the way," Duke asked, "where are you headed?"

"To the Bales cabin. Theron is sick."

He motioned her on and she looked back just once, hoping she would never see him again.

Theron Bales! Duke rolled his eyes as she rode out of sight. Theron Bales had joined Colonel Hoskins' Twelfth Kentucky Infantry but was home on leave.

And Theron Bales' home was where he was headed before crossing back over the border.

CHAPTER NINETEEN

MARNIE HAD returned home from checking on Bessie Harmon and her baby the next day. It had finally become known that her young husband, Stephen, was the courier to Confederate Captain Bledsoe concerning the arrest of Confederate sympathizers in September. Clay had reservations and Mae grumbled about her going to the Harmon home, but Marnie ignored their protests as usual. She had set about helping Mae and Judith with dinner when Clay burst through the back door, face florid and his hat askew.

She had seen that look many times before and knew it foretold of some news about the war. Sighing, she went back to the task of rolling the biscuit dough on the counter in front of her. She didn't want to hear any more bad information of what was going on in the county. When in the world would they hear of anything good?

"Have you heard the news?" barked Clay.

Mae had the oven door open, basting a roast they were having for dinner. From her bent over position, she asked, "What news?"

Looking at Judith, he then asked Mae, "Do you have a bit of milk to give me? I'm thirsty."

Mae's brows drew together, and understanding that Clay didn't want Judith present, closed the oven door and asked Judith to fetch milk from the springhouse.

She left and Clay whipped off his hat and slapped it against his leg in agitation.

“Theron Bales is dead!” he cried.

Mae and Marnie turned and spoke in unison, “Dead?”

“How can this be?” said Marnie, confused and upset that a patient she had just called on the day before was dead. She never liked losing a patient and though sick, it never occurred to her that he was that sick. “Theron had contracted the measles,” she explained, “and I doctored him for a setback, but he wasn’t sick enough to die.”

“Well, let me tell you, missy, he didn’t die of the measles,” he said with emphasis and waited a bit.

Marnie threw her floured hands opened wide. “Well, for goodness sake, are you going to tell me or not?”

“It was like this. According to Theron’s wife and the boy that Theron had working for him—oh, what was the lad’s name?” Putting his finger to his head, he struggled to remember. “Andy something or other. Yes, that’s it. Andy Meece, Lloyd Meece’s grandson. That’s what the boy’s name is. Well, it’s like this—Andy said Theron’s wife was sitting at the open door peeling apples, when Duke came riding up, dismounted, and she asked him to come in and have a chair. He told her he didn’t have time. She then offered him some apples to which he said he had already had some. He then asked about Theron. She told him he was in bed sick, very sick with the measles.”

Marnie’s hand unconsciously gripped the back of the chair.

“Andy was in the next room—Theron’s room alone, evidently trying to talk some business to him. Duke entered the room and went over to the bed and asked Theron if he had been to Camp Dick Robinson. Well, what was Theron going to answer? No? Yes, sir, let me tell you, that’s exactly what he said! He denied it! But what did Duke do? I’ll tell you what he did! He shot him, not once, but twice!” and Clay thumped one fist into the palm of the other hand.

The women were astonished, their eyes large with shock. Marnie’s face did not change—but it was a stunning blow dealt without warning. And as such, in the first moments of shock, she did not realize what had happened.

Theron. Hot-tempered little Theron. The man wasn't over five feet five inches, and he was not much older than she, but hard as a tack and always in the thick of things. A crusader of right, he feared no man and now he was dead.

Marnie was too bewildered and paid little attention to what Clay was thundering on about...'war' or some such thing.

"Pa," Marnie finally interrupted. "What of his wife Anne and Andy?"

"His wife ran away and so did the boy. Andy saw Duke later on that day and ran into a neighbor's house. Duke demanded the woman of the house send him out. He did just what Duke said. Duke pointed his pistol at the boy and then holstering his pistol, cursed and said 'You're beneath my notice' and rode away.

"This is not to be borne, let me tell you. To kill a man when he's sick and lying in bed, and it's not to be borne!"

Judith came in with a pail of milk, and filling a glass, handed it to Clay.

At the questioning look on Judith's face, Marnie felt it best to tell her. Judith had little to say save a flicker of fear in her eyes.

Clay began rambling on again, unshackled by secrecy to Judith.

"In my opinion," he began. "It was not just because Theron joined the Union army. It was about the arrest of Southern sympathizers in this county, as Duke was one of them."

Realizing what he just said, he looked sharply at Marnie, and had to admit she was correct about that ordeal. They should not have rounded men up like that and arrested them and, looking embarrassed, he confessed she was right.

Marnie sat slowly down in a chair. She had a moment of realization. All the things Seth had been warning about were coming true. Things she tried to cast to the side as having no merit.

Now, with the killing of Theron Bales, the Confederates would be more emboldened than they already were. The Union troops were above the Cumberland River, leaving them defenseless but for the Home Guard, and there were precious few of them left. Mostly old men and young boys now made up the male population of Clinton County.

Perhaps she should take Judith and go back home…Mae, too, if she wanted to or if she could convince her to. But, no, she decided, Mae would never leave here. She had traveled with her husband from Virginia to settle in Clinton County years ago. He had died and she became housekeeper to Clay and Marnie. She was too old now and had been with Clay too long to uproot herself.

She looked at Clay's face. In spite of indignation he was portraying, he would never leave here and take her home. He had become too much, the last forty years, like the hill people here, and she dared not try the trip without the protection of men for there were Union and Confederate soldiers alike milling about throughout Kentucky.

This war had given a purpose to Clay's life, the likes he had not had in a long time, not since his wife died. Also, a champion for what is right, he and Theron Bales were too much alike.

Fear churned suddenly inside Marnie and another man was added to her prayer list. As vocal as he was, she just hoped her father did not die by the enemy's bullet as Theron did. Truly, would Duke Morgan attempt such a heinous deed on her father? Would Duke cold bloodedly kill him just because he stood for the Union? The code of some was, "You might not harm the woman, but you wouldn't hesitate to kill her father, brothers, and sons". And in such a war as this, she was not sure the women would survive such vindictiveness.

Feeling overwhelmed as Clay raged on, she decided she had to have some air though it was chilly outside. Rising from her chair, Marnie walked through the parlor, grabbed a shawl, wrapped it around her shoulders, and moved out the door to the front porch and sat down on the step. What was she to do?

"I must think," she told herself over and over. "I must think."

But thoughts eluded her, her mind rushed here and there. "We could go to the valley," she thought, but no one could summon her as a doctor if she were in hiding. And Clay would not do that anyway, at least on a permanent basis. He would refuse to stay out of the fight.

And Judith. By all means, her daughter needed protection. Any rebel guerrilla could take her and—and—she thought of Bob Witter and shuddered.

Perhaps I was wrong to come back.

A breeze blew up on the crisp fall day. She wrapped her shawl tighter around her and then took note of her hands.

They were still caked with flour…and she had no answers.

CHAPTER TWENTY

MIDMORNING, SEVERAL DAYS LATER, a restless Marnie wandered from room to room, listlessly rearranging anything her fingers touched. It was quiet and she heard the tick of the hall clock. Mae and Judith were baking in the kitchen, side meat simmering on the stove, and occasionally she caught sounds of their talking. Her chores were done and though it was cold outside, she felt shut up in the house. Her cheeks burned when Mae told her that her father had left strict instructions for her not to leave the ranch. Marnie wondered if Seth had anything to do with her father's order, and was tempted to blurt out to Mae that she was a grown woman with two children of her own, but she kept her peace as a silent war raged within her, and she bit her lip to keep her composure.

An urgent, sharp knock sounded at the door, and Marnie crossed the room and opened it to find a young teenage boy standing there on the threshold. Behind him, tethered to the rail, stood a lathered horse that indicated he had come in a hurry and she surmised trouble was afoot.

"Are you the doctor?" he asked.

"Yes, I'm Marnie Cross," she answered. "What is it? What can I do for you?"

"Ma says to come and bring your herbs."

"Who are you, child?"

He winced when she called him *child*, and she realized her mistake immediately.

"I'm Isaac Cable, ma'am."

Cable. Yes, she remembered the Cable family from years ago. A large lot of them, if memory served her right. What was the name of the oldest Cable? Don? No. Dan? Yes! Dan Cable—a charismatic, good-looking man that left a lasting impression on her, as well as others. He had caught many a girl's eye, as well as some of the young matrons in the county.

"Would you happen to be any kin to Dan Cable?"

He looked at her in surprise, then shook his head yes. "My oldest brother, ma'am, and he needs for you to come."

"Well, what's the trouble?"

"He's been shot and needs your help right away."

"Shot!"

Isaac shifted on his feet. "Please, ma'am," he implored. "Don't ask any questions. Just come straightaway if you would."

Immediately she shifted into action. Retrieving her coat and medical bag from her bedroom, and a call to Judith with a hurried explanation, her last thought as she crossed the room was what her father would have to say about her leaving the farm. Well, sick folks came first in her opinion. Let Pa say what he wants to. She hastily wrote him a note, placed it on table, and left.

A strong windstorm had the swept the county a few nights ago, evidenced by debris from trees lying on the floor of the woods. The forest light shifted, shrouding them in darkness as they rode through. She could not remember exactly where the Cable farm was located in the county and was impatient to get there. She could not understand why Isaac was keeping to the forest and not the road. With his brother in a precarious physical state, it would certainly be quicker that they ride out of the forest.

"Isaac!" she called. "Why not take the road?"

He looked quickly around at her, and said, "Bushwackers, ma'am. They're about and it's best that you keep your voice down."

Bushwackers? Whatever did Isaac mean? She searched her memory and could not remember Seth or Pa speaking of such people. But, then again, she did not always listen closely to their conversations. Could it be Duke Morgan was a bushwacker?

Isaac suddenly drew up and, hunching down in his saddle, motioned for her to do the same. He turned and put a finger to his lips to silence her. They were not far off the road.

Before long, the sound of horses' hooves approaching, clicking of bridles and straining creak of leather came to her ears, and Marnie sat uncertain in the saddle, peering at a small company of Confederate soldiers riding by. She prayed no soldier would discover them, for though she did not fear for herself, she was afraid for Isaac. Afraid they would harm him in this crazy, mixed up county. Confederates sympathizers afraid of Union folk in Clinton County and Union supporters fearful of Confederates, and sitting astride the horse, she despised it all.

The last of the company passed and Isaac motioned for her to follow him to the road.

"I don't think there's another company this close," he informed her, "however, there may be guerrillas around, but we'll just have to take that risk. I've got to get you to Dan," he said hurriedly.

Arriving at the Cable farm, they turned and rode down a long avenue of trees which led to the
two-story house. Though it was mid-afternoon, the windows were shuttered, no horses were in the corral, and no members of that large family came to usher her in, and she wondered if she had been brought on a nefarious mission of some kind. Was this a trick? Was the Cable family Confederates? It made little difference to her, one way or another, but the residents of the county were zealots of both sides and she did not want to be identified as an enemy to either. She was a doctor, first of all, and had come to heal the sick.

She carefully dismounted her horse, her eyes on the door as she loosened her medicine bag from the saddle, and Isaac led the mounts away, not to the corral as she expected, but rather towards the woods. A shiver traveled down her spine as she cautiously stepped on the porch, but before she took another step, the door opened and Mrs. Cable motioned her in, and, as Marnie crossed the threshold, she took Marnie's arm, pulling her in with haste and hurriedly closed the door after them.

A younger child, wide-eyed with apprehension, silently studied Marnie from where he stood. She looked at him, her eyes shadowed with worry, and somewhere from within her anger rose. These children were too young to be thrust into such a world that was not their making. Their present should not be marred by danger and fear. They should be carefree, able to venture out of doors without the sense of some great peril that awaited them. Instead, danger seemed to hover all around them.

She nearly stamped her foot with the impotency she was feeling. A sound from Mrs. Cable made her suddenly remember the reason she had come, and Mrs. Cable motioned toward the stairs, and, Marnie, with the boys close behind, followed her.

With the windows shuttered, the house was dark, except for light filtering through, and no lamp was lit. Isaac had not told her any details about the shooting, and she so desperately wanted to know. Felt the situation warranted it, but the questions died on her lips when she entered the bedroom.

The room was in semi-gloom for the shades had been pulled down to shut out the brightness. Pinpoints of sunlight came in around the edges, and Marnie could see the room was clean with two beds in it. On a table was a washbasin and pitcher of water.

There, lying in the middle of the narrowest bed was Dan Cable, unconscious from his wound. Though he was a few years older than she, she could tell he still retained his good looks. Powerful shoulders projected from the quilt covering him, black, wavy hair which had not been touched by gray. She had forgotten how good looking he was, and chastened herself for being distracted by his appearance when she was supposed to be on a mission of mercy.

Setting her medical bag on the bed, she placed a hand on his fevered forehead, worry furrowing her own brow. Pulling back the colorful quilt that covered him, she removed the blood soaked towel from his mangled shoulder.

"Mrs. Cable," she said, as she retrieved an instrument from her bag, "I'll need you to boil some water and prepare some bandages while I light a lamp." Marnie glanced at the boys. "And I think it would be a good idea for your sons to keep a lookout for intruders."

Following them down the stairs, Marnie threw Mrs. Cable a questioning look as she stood in the middle of the kitchen.

"What's the matter?" Marnie asked.

Mrs. Cable threw wide her hands. "I'm afraid if I build a fire, someone will see the smoke and we could become attacked."

"Well," Marnie said after some thought. "You can't just stop living. We'll have to take a chance and make a fire. If we don't, Dan could very well lose his arm, and perhaps his life. Have you any Confederate sympathizers in this neck of the woods?"

"There's Luther Goddard down the road a ways, but he's a good-hearted man," she offered. "Though he stands for the South, he feeds Confederate and Union soldiers alike."

"By the way, where is Mr. Cable?"

"He's out with the Home Guard, and it's no telling when he'll be back," she said tersely.

At that answer, Marnie glanced sharply at her face. Was it possible that Mrs. Cable felt as she did about the war? If so, how many other women were feeling that same way at this particular time?

"Never mind," she said instead. "Let's get the fire going."

Sweat wrinkled her brow, but Marnie kept on, attempting to stay the bleeding, and at last extracted the ball from Dan's shoulder. At least it had not shattered the bone. Cleaning the wound with the corn liquor she had asked for and applying snake root to the wound, she looked approvingly at Mrs. Cable. While holding the lantern, not once did the light sway in her hand. Perhaps, having borne so many children, she was used to mishaps that often happened in a large family.

The bandage turned scarlet, and pulling it free she applied a fresh one. Giving her a sidelong glance, Marnie asked, “What exactly happened to Dan?”

Setting the basin of bloodied water on the table, Mrs. Cable remarked, shrugging one shoulder. “Who’s to tell? All I know is that Dan has some position with the Federal army and he wound up here with that shot in his shoulder. If you’re still here when he comes around, you’re welcome to ask him.”

Mrs. Cable’s face was grave as she watched her son, ashen-faced, lying in the bed.

“Will he be all right?”

Marnie reassured her with a slight smile. “He’s strong. And the wound is clean. No bone was shattered. I’ll reapply the bandages. He’s lost a lot of blood and rest is all he needs right now.”

“But the fever—“

“I’ll try and break the fever with boneset.”

“You--you’ll stay, won’t you?”

“Of course. For as long as he needs me.” And with that said, Marnie thought about her father. He would be worried, of course, but she hesitated to send Isaac back with a message. For if something happened to him, as young as he is, she would never forgive herself.

The boys had given up their bed to her, choosing to sleep in front of the fireplace downstairs. During the night, Clarence Cable came home, and, upon hearing the news about Dan, immediately made his way up the stairs. Marnie had determined to stay awake in case Dan worsened and needed her, but had nodded off and awoke with a start when Clarence burst into the room without any pretense of quiet, stepping quickly to Dan’s bedside.

Clarence Cable was a tall man, massive shoulders straining his shirt. "How is he?" he demanded, turning to her, his face grim. Tension was etched into his facial features which had become common place among the men in the county with all the fighting between the Union and Confederates.

Pushing back the quilt that covered her, Marnie climbed out of bed, fully clothed, but felt a chill in the room. Taking a shawl from the bed and placing it around her shoulders, she padded in her socks to Dan's bed, and felt his brow.

Marnie adjusted the quilt around him and then reached for her medicine satchel for boneset for tea. "He's still fevered, which is normal for his wound," she informed Clarence. "He'll be sick for a few days, though. I'll stay with him for a while and try to break the fever. I do have a favor to ask of you, though."

He looked at her askance, and then said, "Anything in my power."

The candle by Dan's bed was nearly spent and she set about lighting a new one.

"Please send word to my father of my whereabouts, what has happened, and that I am safe. I don't want him to come looking for me."

Safe! Clarence Cable silently scoffed. *Who is safe nowadays with this county in Unionist hands one week and Confederate the next?* But instead, answered with a nod and, "Will do."

CHAPTER TWENTY-ONE

SOMETIME IN THE NIGHT, just before dawn ushered in the pale yellow light of day, Marnie awoke to Dan thrashing about, attempting to get up. Once again, she threw back the quilt, and hastened to his bed, a cry of alarm escaping her lips. Worried, she pushed him back.

"Please—you're hurt. You'll reopen that wound in your shoulder."

Catching her hands, he shook his head, and then looked at her through glazed eyes.

"Must—" he uttered through fevered lips, "Must leave. If they find me here—Goddard—down the road."

He struggled as he unfolded to his full height, then staggered and sat back down.

"You must rest," she said, as his head rested in his hands. "You're not able to travel just yet."

"Water. Please give me some water."

Marnie turned away and poured him a cup of water. He drank it down and asked for another.

"Let me help you back into bed and I'll tend to your wound."

He looked down at the bloodied bandages and nodded. "First," he pointed to the corner, "hand me my rifle."

She understood and didn't argue. In his weakened state he wanted his weapon at hand to defend himself.

She helped him into bed, his rifle by his side, and as she sat on the bed and removed the dressing, he watched her as she worked.

"Are you a doctor?"

She smiled. "Some say I am."

"I know you, don't I?" he asked after careful scrutiny.

She nodded a bit absently, her attention fixed on his shoulder.

"I would say you do. I was Marnie Spencer to you…I am now Marnie Cross."

"Clay Spencer's daughter?" Wonderment was in his voice, though weakened by the surgery.

"Yes."

Her blonde hair was spilling over her shoulder and he was tempted to reach up and touch it, if he had the strength, that is. He remembered her well. Remembered seeing and hearing of her when she, as a girl, traveled throughout the county with herbalist Granny Forbes, tending to the sick. She was just about the only girl that had not taken on about his good looks. That very fact intrigued him and he had been tempted to woo her but she only had eyes for Seth McCord at that time.

"You haven't changed much," he told her.

She thought of Judah and Benjamin. This whole ordeal had aged her in a sense and she often wished she could escape from it all.

"Time changes us all," she said, a trace of bitterness in her voice.

"Not that much for you. You were pretty then, still pretty now."

Marnie glanced quickly at Dan. Fevered as he was, and that he could still speak that way to her was a surprise, and her face held a flicker of amusement.

"I think, sir, you are talking out of your head," she told him as she finished.

Although with effort, he gave a playful smile, "No more than usual."

He studied her and something in his look seemed to ignite a mixture of emotions within her, giving her a guarded feeling. How so odd that look reminded her of Judah! She was perplexed for he did not resemble Judah in any way. Judah had brown hair, was a tall man, yet not over six feet. Dan was well over six feet tall with hair as black as a raven's wing. Yet his eyes were green while Judah's were brown.

Her breath caught. What was happening here, and what was this attraction that she was feeling? Marnie was puzzled at her own feelings and tried to find a meaning for them. She looked away, confused.

Her feelings were so tangled she felt she couldn't unravel them.

"Where have you been living all these years?" he asked, after a bit.

"In Green River Country, a place called Stone Valley, and please don't talk anymore."

"Are you referring to Adair County?" he asked, ignoring her request.

"Yes. A place called New Wellington. I'm staying with my father here while the war takes place."

He cleared his throat. "You lived close to Columbia, the county seat?"

"Not too far."

Interest sparked his face and he rallied with strength she thought impossible. "Why, that's pretty much the hub for shipment of supplies to our troops," he exclaimed.

His face suddenly turned grave as though he remembered where he was at. "I can't stay here any longer," he said as he made a feeble attempt to push the quilt aside. "There is danger."

Moving his hand aside and pulling the quilt back over his chest, "I know there is danger," she softly said, emitting a frown from her own forehead. "That's nothing new to anyone in this county," was her wry reply.

Standing up, she looked thoughtfully at his handsome face as her brows knit together in contemplation. *Have you no wife? Why are you alone?*

She sighed. *Just what has he to do with Federal forces? Has he seen Judah? Benjamin? Why had Benjamin not written? Was he captured and taken prisoner?* A deep dread knotted her stomach.

There were so many questions she wanted to ask, and it was on the tip of her tongue to ask them, but, no…right now he needed rest. Dawn was nearly here and tomorrow had become today.

The rumble of thunder sounded in the distance, as storm clouds rolled in and hid the sun of the coming morning.

Washing her hands in the basin and drying them on a clean cloth, she stared out the window at the woods' bare branches. She was worried that someone would show at the house, and silently she hoped the rain would wash out the tracks of Dan's horse. Worry was becoming familiar to her. She worried about family, livestock, Confederates, and just the very fact she was away from home at this moment, in this situation. Wiping her hands on a towel, she turned and studied Dan again. He was strong. She had no doubt he would get well. But in his condition at the moment he was unable to defend home and family.

"Your father is home now," she assured him. "He will know what to do if anyone comes. Sleep…and we will talk later."

His eyes were already closing. He lay back deeper into the pillow, favoring his wounded shoulder. A thought was developing in his mind and Dan was looking forward to their talk, but now he was tired…so very tired.

She looked at his broad shoulders, his muscles relaxed and sleeping now. She wanted to touch him, to put her hand upon his black, wavy hair….

CHAPTER TWENTY-TWO

NOONTIME FOUND MARNIE still sleeping soundly. Try as hard as she could, she had not been able to stay awake. The deep rhythmic sound of Dan's breathing of early morning had subtly drawn her into her own dreams, and for the first time in months she slept without fear, without worry.

She woke to a sound from the window and found the temperature had dropped, and the rain had turned to snow spitting against the window. Rising, she streaked across the room to the window and saw a rising wind whip tree branches, and as she watched, the snow had suddenly gone wild, nearly a whiteout.

Clarence Cable was leading his horses from the corral into the barn and she stayed at the window long after he had emerged, barred the door, and quickly made his way to the house. The first snow of the year, it was, and winter was not far off.

A sigh escaped her lips. She had intended to go home today, but no man or creature would stir in such a storm. She suddenly felt heartened. At least no one would be about looking for Dan Cable.

A noise from the sick bed drew her attention back to Dan.

"What is that sound I hear?" he said thickly, opening his eyes into slits.

"'Tis only a snow storm," she informed him matter-of-factly. "I just woke up myself," she said as she checked his bandage, then laying her hand on his forehead, discovered his temperature had come down and he was only a little warm.

A satisfied look covered her face, and she commented, "Coming along nicely, your shoulder is. You heal quicker than most. Are you hungry?"

"Just a mite."

She smiled. "Well, at least that's the showing of a good sign. I'll go downstairs and see what your mother has for you to eat."

"Will you be going home today?" he asked, an enigmatic look on his face when her hand touched the doorknob.

With a wry smile, she looked back and said, "In this storm? I should say not."

"Good," he said through a smile of his own. "Thank God for the storm."

When Marnie brought his food, Dan ate in silence. He seemed deep in thought about something, and to allow him privacy, she set about preparing more bandages from the cloth Mrs. Cable had given her.

"As there is not much more we can do for the present, shall we have that talk now?" he said after she had set his bowl on the stand.

Giving him a cup of cider, she asked, "Are you sure you are up to it?"

"The sight of you, dear lady—or should I call you doctor?—is enough to rally my senses to its full capacity."

"My, my!" she exclaimed. "What a ladies' man you are!"

Taking a drink, he replied, "Not so much. It's been a long time since—"

Finishing the cider with a gulp, he handed the cup to her. He ran his hand over his stubbled face as though to quell the thought.

Dare she ask him what had been a burning question in her mind?

Swallowing hard, she asked him softly, "You are not married?"

He leaned back against the pillow propped against the headboard. "Not now, I'm not."

Divorce was unthinkable, but was it possible that he was?

"Are you divorced?"

Dan looked at her, eyebrows lifted. "No. My wife died many years ago."

"Oh," she said. "I'm sorry. I didn't mean to bring up an unhappy memory."

He considered her remark. "I don't remember anything unhappy about Mary. As a matter of fact, you remind me of her some."

"I remind you of your wife? Did she have blonde hair?"

He looked at her without emotion. He inspected her hair, her face, and then eyes drifted down the length of her.

"Her hair was dark, just about like mine. She had dark eyes, too."

"But if she was dark and I'm fair?"

"You mean why you remind me of her?"

"Yes."

"I don't know, rightly. She didn't cower at things like some women…took them head on. A certain confidence she had about her, I guess. Something I see in you."

Face flushing a little, her hand touched the rifle and she quickly changed the subject. "It's a fine rifle, indeed."

"Spencer Repeater," he told her, pride in his voice.

"How many shots?"

"Eight."

The Home Guard had trouble getting any basic artillery from the Federal government at all. How did he acquire such a fine weapon? she asked herself.

"How did you happen onto such a rifle as this?"

He ignored her question, asking his own, instead. "This county has been split in politics as you probably well know." She did some ignoring herself for she didn't want to talk about the war.

He pressed her. "Just where do you stand in this war?"

"Me?" She looked away from him. "I—I—if you must know, I stand for neither side."

"And your husband…what's his name?"

Dan was so direct she had half a notion not to answer him at all.

However, she relinquished and answered, "Judah. Judah Cross."

Judah Cross! Doctor Judah Cross! He is with Wolford's Cavalry! They had just had a narrow escape from Confederate Duke Morgan and his band of outlaws. Dan nearly told her this bit of news, but then decided this information he would keep from her, for it would serve no purpose and would only cause alarm.

Feigning ignorance, he asked, "How does he feel about all of this?"

She didn't want to be reminded right now of Judah's departure. "What does it matter?" she stated tersely.

Dan sensed he had hit a sore spot with her. His voice dropped lower…softer. "It matters more than you know."

Marnie sighed deeply. "He's enlisted with the Union as a field doctor." Her face suddenly frowned. "My son, Benjamin, is with the Cavalry, too. Just where he is, I don't know."

"I see. Where is your husband at the present?"

"I—I don't know. I haven't heard from Judah since he left in May, and Benjamin left in August. Frankly, I don't know if either of them is still alive."

No word since May!

"They're alive," said Dan matter-of-factly.

Marnie's head jerked and she stared at him. "They're alive? How do you know?"

"I know. My—position with the army—well, let's just say, I am privileged to know certain things."

She opened her mouth to further pepper him with questions, but he held his hand up silencing her.

"So…you are a doctor."

She did not answer but thought, "Why will he not tell me about Judah and Benjamin? Are they on some secret mission?"

"And you travel around the county tending the sick?" he asked, interrupting her thoughts.

"Whenever I am called, I do," she absently answered.

"And neither Confederate or Union question you at all?"

"They did, at first. But they've got quite used to me going about the county. I minister to the sick, whether Union or Confederate. That is my duty."

Dan led Marnie to talking of her life, how she had ended up a doctor.

"My father was a great believer in children being given responsibility. When I travelled around the county with Granny Forbes, Mae was not so much against it, but when Granny passed away, and I went about on my own, Mae insisted that I stop. However, Pa, feeling that I was doing some good, overrode any objections that she had. After that, I met and married Judah and worked with him in the medical profession."

He regarded her in a thoughtful way, as if sifting every word before he spoke.

"I have a request to ask of you…something I've been thinking about while lying here."

Marnie hesitated a little and then said, "Then, ask it."

"I need your help in something."

Puzzled, she stared at him. She was doing all she could to help him at the moment and it wouldn't be long before he would be completely out of bed.

Dan ran his finger over the bridge of his nose. "It's something rather dangerous, but I believe you're woman enough for it."

CHAPTER TWENTY-THREE

"I'M A UNION SCOUT," he told her when she didn't answer.

His eyes measured her, searching, trying to gauge her response.

"That is privileged information," he said, looking keenly at her.

She shrugged her shoulders. "So why are you telling me this?"

"I want you to work with me," he said quietly, then restated, "I *need* you to work with me."

Her eyes turned incredulous as they searched his. "What do you mean, 'Work with you'?"

His tone turned slightly eager and without thought he placed his hand on hers. "In your position as doctor you can feed me any information about Confederate activity you see in the county. In turn, I can relay it back to Federal Forces about the whereabouts of the enemy."

Marnie was stunned and for a moment her mind was incoherent. She tried to process what he had just said, however, it didn't sink in right away.

"Don't you see?" Dan continued. "This is perfect. Not only are you a doctor, but a woman, also. They would never suspect you. You can move about freely, openly, whereas, I…in the eyes of the Confederates, I am a marked man. I must be very cautious as I move about."

She studied him, concern tightening her features while unconsciously withdrawing her hand as he studied her in return.

What was this insane thing he was asking of her? "Me—a spy for the Union Army?" Her face was full of questions.

"I—I—" she began, and then stopped, contemplating the uncertainties before her.

Confederates had already been to their home two times the last couple of months, albeit without harm, except for stealing a few chickens and their hogs. If they should get wind of this, what would this do to her family, and perhaps ultimately to her? She had enjoyed a great deal of clemency, even as Reverend Jesse Sewell passed back and forth across enemy lines without harm, preaching to both Union and Confederate soldiers.

She thought of Judith. How could she possibly risk her own daughter's life and the life of her father and Mae? And what would Seth McCord say of this?

She rose from the bed and began to pace the floor while Dan waited expectantly for her answer. After several moments she stopped and said, "I'm no soldier, Dan. I have not wanted to get involved in this war on any account. Besides that, I cannot risk my daughter's life. Should they find out that I'm doing this, they will kill us all."

Dan lay in thought for a few minutes. It would not be easy to enlist Marnie to the cause. A younger woman, yes, would be an easy thing to do. However, she was in her forties, mature, and would have more restraint, which on one hand was in her favor. And, yet, what kind of man would ask a woman to do what he was asking? Should she be discovered, she could possibly be killed. Did the war demand the lifeblood of its women as well as its men?

He watched her as she paced the floor, his face somber as he struggled to reconcile the necessity against the danger.

"Do you have family in Adair County?" he finally asked.

Marnie looked at him suspiciously. "Yes. My Grandfather and Grandmother Spencer. They live on an estate called *North Star*."

Dan nodded in thought. "I've heard of it from somebody. Probably Clay."

“I don’t know about this, Dan,” sudden doubt clouding her voice. “They are in their nineties now, and I’m not sure how things are faring at home just now with this war going on.”

“You don’t have to worry, Marnie. Federal troops control that area,” he said in a placating tone. “Think about it, your daughter would be safer in Adair County than here. You have to agree that sending her to them would be better for her as well as solving our problem here.”

“Just how would I go about doing that, if you don’t mind telling me?” Marnie said incredulously. “On any given week, the Confederates control this county, that is, when the Federals don’t mind making a swoop down here and run them out for a bit,” she said, a bit sharply. “And I’m not about to put Judith in danger by taking a chance that they won’t spot you and me together, if that’s your plan.”

Dan chewed on the inside of his cheek in thought for a while. He could see her point.

“I’ll tell you what I will do,” he said. “I’ll send word and find out exactly when they’re coming…then you can send your daughter away at that time.”

“But Judith can’t go by herself!” she protested as she shook her head in denial. “She needs someone to take her and I don’t want to entrust her to strangers.”

“Your father could take her.”

“Pa?” She rolled her eyes. “He’ll never leave that place of his, not even for Judith. He would keep her at—”

Marnie nearly said “his valley” but caught herself in time. No one knew of their hiding place and her father would be furious to know that she divulged it.

“Well, then, what about Seth McCord?” he asked. “He’s one of the few not serving right now.”

She laughed, but she was not amused. “Seth? I doubt that he would leave Clinton County and travel up there. He knows no one in Adair County and has no reason to go.”

She thought, if Seth McCord were around after things escalate, and me still traveling the county in spite of the trouble, there would be endless arguing. And the travesty of it would be, her father might agree with him.

"If you could get Seth to take her home to Adair County, I'll consider it."

Dan swiftly ordered his thoughts and gestured impatiently. "Leave it to me," he said, as though things were settled between them. "I'll request the army send him on some mission to Adair County and he can take her with him."

His abruptness shocked her. Did he really have that much sway with the higher ups of the Federal Army? She looked up and their eyes met. Something in his gleamed a little too warm and hers fell swiftly away.

She felt she was being carried away in a current that was too swift to swim against, and the feeling frightened her just a little.

He said he needed her. Marnie's mind rehearsed their conversation. To work with him would not be as simple as Dan tried to imply. In fact, it was downright complicated. In fighting for the Union would she possibly get hurt? Or would God reward her in doing this thing by bringing Judah back to her? And just whose side was God on anyway?

Marnie walked to the ice-encrusted window, staring at nothing in particular to organize her thoughts. Isaac was breaking the skim of ice off a bucket of water by the back door. Seeing her standing at the window watching him, he waved and she returned his gesture. This war was hard on the children. Judith had no social life to speak of, and was nearly a prisoner on the ranch. What was going on at *The Crossing*, she'd had no further word. Adair County may not be much better than this, but she decided that was a chance she had to take. If working with Dan was what it took to get Judith out of the terrors of Clinton County, then she would.

Very carefully she schooled her emotions and turning back to him, said, “All right, then, Dan. Make the arrangements. I’ll work with you…as long as Judith gets safely to Adair County.”

CHAPTER TWENTY-FOUR

WHAT ON EARTH had she agreed to do? Work with him? Work with him?

How could she work with him? Just looking at him muddled her emotions to where she couldn't think straight. Dan had talked so persuasively, that by the time he was done, she was ready to say yes to almost anything. In all her acquaintances, she had never met anyone so captivating in her life.

Riding home alone the next morning, she began to suffer misgivings about her word she had given him. She was worried about Judith. How could Dan possibly arrange to get Seth McCord out of the county? Seth had been in the Home Guard, yes, but would never join regular army. He didn't share the passion, as others did, of the worthiness of going to war, although he wasn't exactly against it. He took it merely as a circumstance that had come to Clinton County and one that must be dealt with.

Truly, Seth was wise enough to possess foresight to anticipate what was in the future for the county, but he wasn't doing as others have done. Many families had pulled up stakes and moved elsewhere. Looting was becoming a common occurrence in Albany, as Confederate guerrillas and sometimes soldiers inhabited the town.

A sad sight it was, several buildings standing empty when previously it was prosperous and busy. Confederates inhabited

Albany most of the time now when the Federal Army wasn't around. The court house was empty now, bespeaking of a time when there was law and order. Soldiers stationed themselves there now.

It was a slow ride back to the ranch, for wherever she looked she saw the image of Dan Cable, recovering in bed. When he stood, she barely came to his shoulder, so tall he was. His presence was overwhelming at times, and he had an air of self-confidence about him that spilled over to her and made her feel secure.

But on this cold morning, snow still wrapped the trees like a winter coat and lay like a blanket on the ground. Nature was incredibly still, weighted with silence, and all she heard was the soft hoof falls of her horse in the snow. She was alone and in her aloneness she did not feel so confident. Riding a horse alone, as Marnie was doing right now, was a time for thinking, and again her thoughts turned to Judah, and she wondered just where he was at the present. At least he was alive!

What Dan was asking of her, she felt no other man would expect. But Dan's faith in her inspired her, and she felt a certain reverence about it. It reminded her of the camaraderie between Judah and herself. Judah believed in her and was proud of her ability in the medical field, and they were as one in surgery.

Dan had spoken of the working relationship between the opposite genders. He had said, "This is as it should be…a man and a woman working toward something. Not apart…but a team."

Certainly not the thinking of Seth McCord, and recalling him set her about scoffing again. Seth treated her at times as though she was a mindless child and that irritated her immensely. His constant bickering and ordering her about weighed heavy on her at times…not that she heeded much to his advice.

Credit she must give to her father, for he allowed her to tend the sick even though he worried about her and drew the line where Seth was concerned.

Marnie was thinking too much of the uncertainties before her, as was her usual custom to do. That was the one thing Judah never understood about her. Perhaps it was just a female trait, but she wanted to know the why, how, what and where about everything. She took things apart in her mind and tried to sensibly put them in perspective to her point of view.

At this point in time, Dan and Judah were synonymous in her mind and she realized that was a dangerous game to play, for Judah was not here to defend himself.

A bird flew up, sailed away a few yards, and then vanished into the brush, breaking the silence, startling her.

She needed to get her head straight.

Lord, help me.

For the first time since Marnie agreed to work as a spy, Dan Cable, Seth McCord, and a courier with Dan, appeared at their door early one morning. It wasn't in the heart of Clay Spencer to turn down a fellow Union man and ordered Mae to prepare a fine breakfast for the 'boys in blue'.

Standing in the parlor, Dan told Clay the reason for his visit.

The army was seeking horses for the Union, he told Clay, and as Clay was well known for his fine horseflesh, Dan indicated he had the authority to purchase, and the army would pay handsomely for his mounts.

Noticing the absence of the horses about the place, Dan asked as to their whereabouts, if they had been stolen as so many others had, and Clay sputtered a cough and finally admitted they were hidden where no one could find them.

Though sometimes easily swayed, Clay was nevertheless a shrewd man. And where his daughter was concerned, his actions were not for a lack of sharp-wittedness. It was merely that he could deny her nothing, even sometimes that which was not entirely for her good.

Something was not quite right, his intuition was telling him. Oh, he believed Dan when he said the army needed horses, for horses were nearly as valuable as men, for often as many horses were killed in battle as men were.

No…it was something else, and as Dan talked, Clay tried to put his finger on just what it was. He didn't like feeling this way as though something was out of joint. He had no qualms about selling his stock, for that had been his business for years. Known for the superiority of his horses, when anyone purchased from Clay Spencer, he bought quality. Something was riding him, something—

Dan was not a purchasing agent or with the commissary department…that he was sure of. Yet, here he was, one of the toughest men, one of the best shots known for his marksmanship in the county, buying horses. The army would not waste its time using such a man in this position. There were other ways of using his skill. Something just didn't quite fit.

After negotiations, Clay finally agreed to part with the majority of his herd…after all, the Union needed them.

"How are you going to drive them to Columbia?" inquired Clay. "With the Confederates in Albany right now, there's no way you can pass through them."

"There are no Confederates in Albany at this time."

"You know of that, for certain?"

"Yes, sir."

"You'll be driving them yourself, then?"

"No. Seth here will be taking them to Columbia."

"Seth? He—"

Seth interrupted suddenly. "I'll be taking them, Clay," he explained. "The Union is buying my stock also and Colonel Wolford requested that I deliver them. They're needed for his cavalry."

Clay's eyebrows rose in surprise. "I didn't know you were personally acquainted with Colonel Wolford, Seth."

"I'm not, Clay, but—" And looking at Dan, his words trailed off.

"Let me explain, Mr. Spencer," Dan interposed. "There is a man in Wolford's cavalry that has referred you as a man that could supply what they need. His name is Benjamin Cross. Your grandson, I believe."

Marnie jerked her head in his direction. Benjamin! With Wolford's cavalry! And when she wanted information from Dan about Benjamin, he denied her. All these months she wondered and worried and prayed. For a moment she smoldered with pain. And she had agreed to work as a spy with him!

Dan avoided her look and said to Clay, "However, there is some other news I have that is important for you to know.

"Confederate General Zollicoffer is moving thirteen regiments and a battery to Camp McGinniss in Tennessee, within a few miles of the state border. They'll be crossing soon. Their final destination I'm not at liberty to reveal at the present, but if we're going to get these horses moving, it must be done now, sir."

"Seth will need more men," said Clay. "Do you have the men to move them?"

"We can gather a few—but I have a further request of you."

Something more than the horses? Did he want the rest of the livestock, too?

Reservation on his face, he finally said, "Say on."

"Sir, Marnie would like her daughter to leave at the same time under protection of the men…for her own safety, mind you. And as Seth has agreed to sell and deliver some few horses of his, she would like Seth McCord to accompany Judith back to Adair County."

Marnie had been silent all this time. Clay looked first at Seth, then Marnie with surprise.

"I didn't know," with brows drawn together in suspicion, he addressed Marnie, "you had been planning all of this."

"I didn't really," Marnie answered, "but it's been on my mind these last few days. "Don't you see, Pa," she pleaded, "the danger that is coming with Zollicoffer's men so close to our county, it is crucial that Judith get away. Send her to *North Star* to Grandfather Spencer's. She'll be safer there."

Clay gnawed on his lower lip for a moment in thought. Could it be that something was between Seth and Marnie, and that something was in the making? Was she divorcing Judah for Seth? Was this what he was feeling? He loved her with all his heart, but divorce was something he wouldn't stand for.

Looking her straight in the eye, his own meanwhile accusing, "And, is it, missy, that you will be going with Judith and Seth?" he asked Marnie.

"No, Pa. I'm staying here with you and Mae, and for the people who need me as a doctor."

Admiration lit up his eyes. His only child…willing to stay with her father in such a time of trouble, with Confederates invading the county, rather than thinking of herself. What a chip off the old block, she was, and so much like his own mother Rachel.

"Is this what you're wanting then, for Judith to leave with Seth, for certain?"

"Yes, Pa. You can't leave," she reasoned, confidence in her voice, Just the very fact that she had a plan gave her confidence and a feeling of greater security. "I can't leave, either. I want someone along with Judith that she knows. Not just with a bunch of rough strangers…begging your pardon," she indicated with a nod of her head toward Dan.

"You're in agreement with this, Seth? You'll escort my granddaughter back to North Star?"

"I will, Clay."

"Do you not realize there may be trouble between here and there? Sesech are not just in our county, you know."

"I'm aware of that, Clay. But the men that Dan will provide me with will be adequate, I'm sure, and I'll be taking Ed with us."

Clay's brow furrowed and he looked doubtful. He wouldn't want anything to happen to his only granddaughter. She was not of the temerity that Marnie was. Marnie had nerve—too much at times, but Judith was gentle and reserved. He supposed the cheekiness that Marnie possessed was the way he had raised her, and had, in secret, been proud of. Though repulsed by Duke Morgan, he owed his thanks to Duke. Marnie had had relative safety from the Confederates…but Judith?

If Seth had been a careless man, Clay would not consider it for a moment. But he knew him to be level-headed and cautious.

Dan spoke up. "I've already dispatched men to meet us outside of Albany."

Clay asked, "You were that sure I would sell?"

Dan grinned. "You're a Union man, aren't you?"

"I'll take care of her, Clay," Seth promised, dispelling any doubts Clay had. "She'll make it to North Star."

Not one to linger about making a decision, Clay suggested that Dan accompany him and Seth to his valley for horses.

Though the matter was settled, something still did not sit right with him. Just what was it?

Dan and Marnie stood before the fireplace that evening instead of sitting. She had wrestled all day about the fact that Dan had withheld knowledge about Benjamin. And then there was Judah. Dan said he was all right, too. What exactly was so secretive that he could not tell her any more than he had? Some strategy kept in secret from the enemy? If that was the case, all she could do was pray.

She felt more at ease now that the matter was settled about Judith. Dan had kept his promise. She would soon be safe at *North Star*, and to that, Marnie was grateful.

The firelight illuminated his face. Rugged lines were pronounced indicating an especially rough and dangerous life he was living. Scouting for the presence of the enemy, often the necessity for finding shelter in the forest or some cave somewhere from the cold and rain. Yet those lines on his face made him all the more striking and she felt herself drawn to him.

All that evening, he had been looking for an opportunity to speak to her alone, but Clay had been with him constantly talking war and war business.

After Seth had left, and Clay retired to bed, he finally had her alone.

His face was inscrutable, and she couldn't tell what he was thinking.

He turned to her then and caught her studying him. Embarrassed, she took the poker and jabbed it against a log that was not quite ready to fall.

"Marnie," he began thoughtfully and softly.

She looked at him with questioning eyes.

Her son Benjamin was sick in camp with a case of the measles. How could he tell her that knowing that that disease sometimes killed the most stalwart of men?

He swallowed hard and she could see his throat tighten.

No, he decided, he would not tell her. She would be like a she-bear when her cub was in danger. She would throw all caution to the wind and leave immediately and go to him in spite of danger lurking about. And if anyone tried to restrain her, she would sneak away at the first opportunity, probably follow along behind Seth at a respectable distance to Adair County. She would know soon enough, should he not live. And should he not—he couldn't think of that right now knowing what it would do to her.

He said, instead, "Please be careful. I don't want anything to happen to you."

It was sunrise. The shadows in the yard drew back, hiding under the porch. Dan strolled to the corral to lean on the rail, watching the horses. They stirred warily, yet one stopped suddenly, ears pricked, and was looking at him. "Come here, boy," he said softly, and to his surprise the dappled gray came. "It's all right, boy," he whispered and held out his hand.

The horse's nose extended, sniffing the fingers.

"You have a way with horses, Dan."

He turned to find Marnie at his elbow. "Your father has some fine horseflesh here."

“Pa was always known to have the finest horses in the county,” she said, pride in her voice.

“That he has, for a fact.”

Taking his arm from the rail, he turned completely to look at her. “You are a very beautiful woman, Marnie.”

She flushed slightly, but said nothing.

Abruptly she turned and went back to the house. Whatever she had come to say, she had changed her mind. He watched her go, admiring her easy walk.

He had no right to think of this woman. She was married but there was a part of his life needing to be filled. He was inviting trouble he could not afford. He needed to keep his mind clear for the troops depended on the information he could relay to them.

Something stirred deep within him, something forgotten. For the last fifteen years since the death of his wife, he had never pursued another woman, though some had inclined their eyes his way. Never a womanizer, he was a one woman man. He had filled his moments with work, building up his place, following lonely trails where they existed. It had been a long time since he had loved a woman, and with surprise, he realized he was falling in love with Marnie Cross. Was it possible she had feelings for him, too?

What had happened between them that he should feel so sure of what he felt? So little had been said, so little done. Yet there was a deep inner realization that this was the woman with whom he could be happy. Should he survive the war, this was the woman he wanted to spend the rest of his life with. He watched her disappear into the house.

“You’ll make a fool of yourself,” he said aloud, “if you’re not careful.”

CHAPTER TWENTY-FIVE

FOR THE FIRST TIME since the war began the valley folk heard the sound of the tramping of Confederate soldiers. Though bands of soldiers and guerrillas had been a source of terror through this part of the county, the full scale advance was intimidating and panic lay just below the surface.

Dan Cable's information was right. Seth and Judith had been gone but a few days, and they came as he said they would.

Seth seemed relieved to go to Columbia for some of the women in the county and about Albany had turned bitter against any eligible man that was not in Federal uniform, and though Seth was not as young as some recruits, he was still young enough to enlist, with the added fact that he was a single man. The word would get around, as it usually did, that he was driving horses north for the Union cavalry. That would take the sting out of their hatred.

The gray troops passed by farms and cabins attended mostly by women and children and the aged men. And to those being invaded, it seemed to be the whole of the army of 10,000 troops. In reality, if those inhabitants could have known, it was merely part of Zollicoffer's army according to the scouts' report to Colonel Hoskins. They were not inclined to fight at this time, for they were on their way to Mill Springs in Pulaski County to join Zollicoffer and Confederate troops there.

Yet, it was overwhelming for those living in that region. The troops camped on the creeks for miles, breaking rail fences for what seemed like a thousand campfires.

It was this act of destroying fences that riled Clay Spencer beyond any fear he might have had seeing the number of troops.

He stood looking from the window, viewed through his spy glass through the break in the trees, his face growing red, and shifted one foot to another like a restive elephant, seeing no soldiers on his property yet, but hearing the sound as they worked along the creeks. It would not be long.

"By thunderation, I ought to get my rifle and shoot the lot of them!" he declared in a heated moment.

Mae and Marnie begged him to reconsider.

"Pa, if you do that, you'll bring the whole army up here!"

She knew his temper. One shot was all it would take and they would be fired on by the entire army. Funny, at this moment she recalled Grandmother Spencer telling her that though they were twins, Cole was the impetuous one and Clay always calm and cool-headed. In years past that might have been true, but since the war began, Clay was an entirely different man and was too quick to act without reason.

"Pa, why don't you go to your valley?" suggested Marnie.

"Me?" He turned and looked at her as though she had taken leave of her senses. "Turn tail and run like a coward? No. I'll not leave you and Mae here by yourselves to face these rebels. If I go, you go with me."

Me leave? Marnie thought. The notion lay like cold lead in her breast and she looked about at the walls. There were too many memories in this place. Marnie thought of her years of growing up in this house, a vague memory of her mother standing over the stove in the kitchen, and at night, tucking her into bed, singing her to sleep, times that Seth McCord came calling to court her. How could she bear to see it burned to the ground with blackened chimneys left standing like sentinels over its past grandeur?

Marnie said a quick prayer under her breath. “Dear Lord, don’t let them burn down the barn, stables or the smokehouse.”

She turned from her memories and said to Clay, “If Mae and I stay,” she reasoned patiently, “they won’t take over the house when they know we’re here. It looks to me like they’re just passing through. Take the horses with you, Pa. We don’t want the three horses we have here to be stolen—and hurry—gather the chickens. You know how the Confederates are! They’ll take off with everything we have without a by-your-leave and may even burn this house to the ground if you give them any trouble.” She felt a twinge at that. She knew there were Union guerrillas that did the same to Confederate sympathizers in the county, but when she had mentioned it in the past, he had stilled her words, calling them traitorous. And then added that if that was what they were doing, “More power to them”.

“But—” he argued, sounding fretful, “’Tis not right to leave you here.”

“Now, Pa,” she began, trying not to sound urgent, though her mind was saying, ‘Hurry, Hurry’. “You know yourself, if they began burning homes down over our heads, the Union Army would swoop in here in no time. That’s not what they want. Remember, they’re marching to some destination, according to Dan. This is not where they want trouble or to make a stand. Think about it. They would not be on their guard as much if you were here. Get the horses, Pa, take them away,” she said again.

“They’ll take them away from us—and I refuse to give them our horses!” she said swiftly when he stood there in hesitation.

And then she laughed contemptuously in an effort to move him, “And just think what a fine thing it would be, a story you could tell, that you took the animals right out from under their noses and hid them away. The whole Confederate army!”

A twinkle came into his eyes, then.

“You’re right, daughter. But I won’t go as far as the valley. I’ll go to the north pasture where I can watch over you from a distance.”

And, of a sudden, he had his hat and coat and was gone.

Marnie saw Clay disappear to the north pasture and walked back into the house. As she stood in the parlor, she heard coming up the drive the sound of horses' feet, and the jingle of bridle bits and she crossed quickly to the window, hiding behind the curtain. There were two of them on horseback.

"Pray, Mae!" she uttered, her eyes meeting Mae's frightened ones. Fright and worry was written on Marnie's face. For a swift moment there went through her memory the stories that had been told of rape, torture and murder, and her hand unconsciously covered her breasts. Those heinous acts were synonymous in her mind with the thousands of gray uniforms beyond their drive, and she wanted to grab Mae and run out the back door. "I shall die. I shall die," she thought in near hysteria.

She saw them stop and glance around before they cautiously dismounted. Taking their pistols from the holsters, they slowly made their way to the porch.

Mae went to the mantel, took Clay's rifle, extended it for Marnie to take, and hissed "Here!"

Marnie left the window, and, swinging into action, took the rifle with fingers that trembled, positioned it behind the door, and then drawing a deep breath to calm herself, opened it at their knock. If they tried anything, she would kill at least one of them, and no doubt would be killed herself.

There was something familiar about the face of one of the soldiers. Of course! Stephen Harmon! She had delivered his wife's baby, and how hard a delivery that was! So…he was now officially part of the Confederate army! The only safe place, she figured, for him to be, as he was the courier that took word to Captain Bledsoe. And how would he repay her for bringing his son into the world? Burn the house down around them? They had taken most of their provisions on hand at the house. Was that not enough to make Unionists suffer? She could feel swift anger stir.

“Where are your men folks?” asked a sergeant as she held open the door.

His eyes took her in from head to heels in a look that missed nothing, an unclothing glance that stirred inward rage at his impudence, and she half-expected some unseemly remark. And if he did—well, she didn’t know exactly what she would do. One thing she would not do is to encourage him in any way that she had heard some women, as camp followers do. She would not be thought of as a prostitute. She was a lady and expected to be treated as such.

“If he’s waiting for an invitation to enter,” she then thought, her nails digging into her palm, clenching her fist, “he’ll be waiting a long time.”

Ever so slightly, she stiffened and fought to keep her poise. Seeing her anxious face, Stephen gave a slight smile and his eyes were kind. She had one hand on the knob, her heart beating rapidly, ready to slam the door in their faces.

Did her face betray her fear? She gulped once and found her voice. She mustn’t let these Confederates know she was afraid.

“There are none here. Just this lady and myself,” motioning to Mae, however, looking at Stephen.

The sergeant leaned his head forward and looked in the room, but made no effort to step inside, and he acted as though he enjoyed her discomfiture.

“I’ll take your word for it,” he finally said.

Brought up short, Marnie wondered at it all. They weren’t going to make any effort to search the house? They weren’t going to take their possessions? He didn’t even ask if they were Union or Confederate, and the marvel of it was Stephen knew Clay was somewhere about, yet held his peace.

“We’re asking the women in this valley to cook us some food and then we’ll move on tomorrow,” he explained. "It doesn’t matter. Anything you have on hand, if you don’t mind.”

If I don’t mind? For the Confederates?

Love your enemies, bless them that curse you, do good to them that hate you.

Marnie held back a groan. That Scripture was asking a hard thing of her.

"We haven't much here," she said, after recovering her composure. "But perhaps some corn cakes?"

He nodded. "That'll do."

"All right," she said, and started to close the door.

The sergeant put his foot in the door and her heart gave a leap thinking he changed his mind about entering.

"Uh. I've been told you're a doctor, ma'am."

She looked at Stephen again. So that's why Stephen came.

"Yes, I am."

"Well, we could sure use your services. We've got a man that has burned himself pretty bad, and if you could see to him, we'd appreciate it."

Into the heart of the Confederate army? she thought.

"All right. Let me get my medicine chest. I'll be right with you."

As they turned back toward their horses, she closed the door and leaned against it. She was frightened, more frightened than she had ever been. She—Marnie Cross—entering into the enemy's camp!

Lo, I am with you always.

CHAPTER TWENTY-SIX

DUSK CAME SLOWLY to Clay Spencer's ranch. From the far hills, a coyote called. It was nearly December and a cold wind was blowing stiffly.

It was late, Mae had retired for the night, and Marnie was ready for bed, but she was not sleepy. Wistful, from the window, she glanced at the moon, and with a sigh, sat down in front of the fire.

She revisited the memory of moving about among the troops. When it was all over, she could feel their eyes follow her as she took her departure from them. Whatever had these men had on their minds? She walked up the drive, glanced back at the encampment, relief making her woozy.

Wondering where her men were tonight and if they were sheltered from the cold, she heard the sound of music. Someone in the Confederate camp was playing a tune on the fiddle. A fiddle? Were they mad? Who would be crazy enough to carry a fiddle into battle? She would never understand the logic of a man.

Though they had not invaded the house, knowing there was an army of Confederates just below the drive, kept her in a state of anguished apprehension. The only relief she had was the thought that Benjamin was gone and not subjected to this. But even this relief did not free her from the state of dread and her ears were ever alert to any sound outside the door.

She supposed it was Stephen's intervention that she was treated with such politeness and she suspected that he had informed them falsely that they were Confederate sympathizers for he had thanked her for caring for his wife in the presence of the sergeant.

If they thought her family was for the Confederacy, their appreciation didn't extend quite as far as she expected. The soldiers still tore down their fences.

The grass was sorely torn and trampled all through the valley where they encamped. The church! What had they done to the church down the road? She envisioned its sacred doors savagely torn open, its sanctuary desecrated, its altar defiled where she had prayed many a prayer. There were no services being held there now, but surely after the war they would have a preacher again.

Campfires burned high to warm the troops, and amid the fires lighting the valley, there came a scratching on the back door.

Clutching her wrapper about her, Marnie wouldn't open it until she heard her name called. She unlocked the door and opened it, the wind gusting in, banging the door against the wall, blowing out the candle in her hand.

A man pushed her gently aside and closed the door quickly behind him.

With the light out, it was dark. "Marnie," the voice said. It was not the voice of her father, but the voice of Dan Cable.

"Dan!"

He put his finger to her lips to shush her. He grinned in the darkness and said quietly, "You didn't think I'd leave you by yourself at a time like this, did you?"

He wouldn't leave me? Judah did. The sting of betrayal still hurt.

Before she had time to answer, he asked, "Where's Clay?"

"He took the horses to the north pasture."

"Good man."

"But, Dan, you shouldn't be here! They—they might spot you and—"

"They're not going to spot me," he said firmly, moving about the kitchen to shutter the window and shut the curtains. He moved into the parlor lit by the fireplace, and ducking under the window, darkened it from any outside prying eyes. She followed along behind him, sputtering her objections.

He permitted her to light a candle as he shed his hat and coat. "Don't you know I'm good at my job? Besides, they're moving on tomorrow. I'm hungry, Marnie. Fix me something to eat, will you?"

She had a hundred questions to ask him, but he ran a hand over the stubble of a two-day beard and had moved to the washbasin in the kitchen and set about washing his face and hands.

A few corn cakes were left, or rather saved from feeding the soldiers, and she brought out a ham, hidden in the cellar from the Confederates (Thank God, they didn't search the house or the springhouse!). She dared not go to the springhouse for potatoes she had stored in straw. She made a mental note to move them, or most of them to the valley, but how she would store them, she didn't know. There was no springhouse in their valley. Only a small shack redone for emergency leave-taking.

"Did Seth and Judith make it to Stone Valley all right?" asked Marnie as he sat hungrily eating. She hadn't had any word and had been worried.

"They did," he answered, then took a bite of bread.

"Good. I was concerned about them."

A grin appeared on his face.

She rose to get the coffee pot and poured him another cup of coffee.

"What's the smile about?" she asked, setting the pot on the stove.

He looked up from his plate. "Brace yourself. I've got some news. Seth has joined up."

Marnie had looked away. Now she swung her head back and stared at him in wonderment.

"Seth? Enlisted?"

"He did. At Camp Boyle. I guess he got tired of explaining why he was not at the front," he said with a chuckle.

"Camp Boyle? Where's that?"

"Oh, it's a new camp outside Columbia."

"What do you know about that!" and she plumped down in her chair in amazement. "I never thought to see the day that Seth McCord would enlist!"

"I've brought Ed back with me. He's a bit too old for active service and is at Seth's place. Seth wants him to stay here, though, with you and Clay. I need to talk to Clay about it."

"Oh, Pa won't mind and will actually enjoy having Ed here." She smiled. "He'll have someone close to talk to about the war." Her smile turned to a frown. "And it's dangerous for any man to be traveling alone right now."

"No one Seth's age is going to be able to sit out the war. Mark my word. Unless this war ends quickly, every available man will be involved."

"How do you know that?"

"There's no use telling pretty lies. I see and hear things. It is bad in Clinton County right now, but since Tennessee has seceded from the Union and is considered a Confederate State, believe me, they've got their own share of troubles, too, with part still holding to the Union and part to the Confederacy. Fortunately for the Union army, east Tennessee is mostly Unionist, with the Confederate sympathizers in the minority.

"The Unionists are pouring across the border to enlist. As for the rest of Tennessee, some are able to move their families, but others…."

Others, she thought. Others stuck in the same situation they were. The men were afraid to go about the county alone now. Horses, mules, pigs, anything that could be taken were being stolen. The citizens were nearly in dire straits, and should they resist, the marauders did not hesitate to use force or kill.

She told him of her neighbors, the Pendleton family. They had four sons in the Union, and Reuben Pendleton, fearing for the rest of his offspring, packed up and left, moving to Russell County above the Cumberland River.

"It's beginning to happen a lot," he said and nodded in agreement.

Briefly, Marnie outlined the events of the visit from the sergeant and Stephen, and her subsequent treating the soldier, and how startled and frightened she was at seeing so many gray uniforms in one place that stretched for miles.

"I saw you," he confessed. "You didn't seem much afraid."

"You—you were watching me?" she said in amazement.

A smile creased his handsome face.

"Of course."

"But—where—how?"

"I was so close I could nearly reach out and touch you, it seemed. But it does not matter. You were very brave." Admiration was on his face, and it was obvious he was smitten with her.

"Oh, I was afraid all right," she said, her voice thick with conviction.

"You hid it very well. You apparently didn't notice the attention you were drawing."

"What do you mean?"

"The soldiers." He shrugged his shoulders. "Maybe it was because they had never seen a woman doctor, but I don't think that was it."

At the questioning look on her face, he laughed. "You're a very pretty lady." His voice was soft but there was a vibrant note in it.

Before his gaze, her eyes fell in confusion, and to mask her feelings she smoothed a crease on her wrapper.

"Dan," she said, changing the conversation in a different direction, "you must be very careful, coming that close to the enemy. You were shot before, remember?"

He laughed again, reached out to touch her hand, and then, hesitated and picked up his cup instead.

"And I had a very pretty lady patch me up. It was worth it to meet you again."

Marnie looked at him, about to hush his teasing, but there was no mirth in Dan's eyes.

"Pretty women drive a man to desperate measures sometimes," he murmured in a self-deprecating tone. His carefully ordered emotions were suddenly fraying and he dropped his eyes back to his plate. He became disinclined to talk and they sat there in silence broken only by the sound of his eating.

It seemed strange to her, thousands of Confederate troops camped outside and Union scout Dan Cable, unbeknownst to them, sat across the table from her.

He was brooding, and she had learned living with Judah, to leave a man alone when he is in such a state. She suspected Dan's musings had to do with her, and for the sake of their working relationship, she decided to let things lie, and got up and went into the parlor to lay more wood on the fire. She took a seat in the rocking chair, and sat listening to the wind hurling itself out into the night and cast sidelong glances toward the kitchen where Dan sat at the table.

After a few minutes, Dan finished eating and took a final drink of his coffee and joined her. He stood at the hearth, staring into its flames as though its yellow tongues held the answers there to something he was seeking.

The clock on the mantel ticked as steady as a heartbeat and it was nearly midnight. What a day this had been, she, a lone woman, walking among thousands of soldiers with her medicine bag. If they had known she was a spy, they would have arrested her there on the spot.

"Is Duke Morgan among them, you think?" she finally asked, breaking the silence.

Dan's face turned dispassionate and held a question as he looked at her. "The troops out there?"

"Yes."

"No," answered Dan, looking back into the fire. "He's back in Tennessee. This is regular army. He won't be with Zollicoffer."

"Well, I was just wondering—"

"Don't over-think this one, Marnie," he suggested without looking at her. "You are safe, at least for the present. Stay strong. Just check it up to the providence of God."

She looked at him in surprise. This was the first he had spoken of God and wondered if he was a Christian. He had not said a blessing over his food, which was customary. It intrigued her and she wanted to continue in the same vein of conversation, but he was so full of secrets. Was this a secret, too?

Instead, she asked, "Where's your courier?"

"He's gone with information to—" he broke off. "He's gone with information."

There was again a soft knock at the back door and she rose from her chair, and in the kitchen, opened it to Clay.

CHAPTER TWENTY-SEVEN

1862

DAN WAS GONE, had been gone for several weeks, and nearly two months after the Confederates had come through the valley, the news came that the battle at Mill Springs was won by Union forces. The Confederate soldiers that had marched through so confidently before were now hungry, tired, passing through Albany back to Tennessee. As bad as it was in Clinton County right now, the thought that a battle at Mill Springs had occurred only forty miles away, was distressing to residents. Some bushwacking and skirmishes were occurring, thievery was rampant, but a major battle…so near?

A neighbor, John Copley and his son had been to town for the mail and brought back an unexpected letter for Marnie. It was from her Uncle Cole. She trembled with fright, holding the letter to her breast, anticipating bad news. What had happened? Was Judith all right? And Judah and Benjamin. Were they at the battle of Mill Springs? Were they hurt or lay dying somewhere on the battlefield?

"My Lord, don't let them be dead!" she cried in anguish. She laid the unopened letter on the mantel. Fear spawned panic in her. If something were wrong, she—. Her heart pounding, Marnie walked outside and stood on the porch. It was freezing cold and she had left her coat inside. Wrapping her arms about her shoulders for warmth, she argued with herself until reason returned. Better to know than to live with uncertainty.

She returned to the parlor, took the letter off the mantel and with shaking hands, opened it. Sitting in the rocker, she smoothed out the letter on her lap. The room was dim with the cloudy afternoon. So urgent to know what it said, she did not bother to light a lamp, and she held it against the light of the hearth.

Dearest Marnie,

First of all, let me say that Judith is doing well at North Star. She is good company for Mother. Some of the boys working there seem to be quite taken with her and she gets more work out of them than Mother's badgering.

Father and Mother send their regards and tell me they worry about you going about the county on your own, especially in light of the trouble there.

I have seen Judah a couple of times but he seemed quite preoccupied. He never asked about you (perhaps I should not tell you that), but I informed him anyway that you were tending the sick there in Clinton County.

The hospital is full with wounded from Mill Springs. A temporary hospital has been set up at the hotel. I guess you and Judah never thought such a splendid place would ever be used for that purpose, did you? Those convalescing men have never seen such magnificent rooms. I talk in such a manner to you, dear Marnie, because I am distressed at the mangled bodies I see and tend to. Your Uncle Adam is the doctor here, and the ladies about New Wellington have volunteered as nurses, and we are so fortunate to have them as every pair of hands is so desperately needed.

I guess you know that Benjamin has contracted the measles. He is on the mend, though, and doing quite well. They have moved him from the hospital to the hotel to recover as the hospital is needed for surgery.

You would never recognize Columbia now. With thousands of Union soldiers about, it has become the point where supplies and artillery are received and dispensed to the army.

I'm sure you are doing a great deal of good there in Clinton County, but I wish you would consider coming back to Adair County. The hospital and hotel could use your services more than you could ever realize. Would you be willing to come home? Please write—or the very least, telegraph me, should you decide to leave there.

Give my regards to Clay. If you decide to return to Stone Valley, please persuade him to accompany you. Mother and Father have not seen him in a very long time and are longing to look on his face once again.

As always...Your loving Uncle Cole."

Marnie laid the letter on her lap and put her head back against the rocker as thoughts swirled in her head. So Benjamin had the measles. She was sure Dan had known. Why had he not told her? She would have gone speedily to him, soldiers or no soldiers. She would take him to task about that the next time she saw him.

And Judah never asked about her. That hurt. Was it truly over between them now? Even if the war ended tomorrow, had the things she said to him completely severed their relationship?

Should I return to Adair County? she thought. What about the agreement I made with Dan?

The next morning Marnie never discussed the letter with her father. He had seen her so little the last twenty years, she had a feeling he would argue against her leaving the county. She had often wondered why he never married again for he was still a handsome man. She tried to broach him on the subject once, but he had become so agitated she thought he would box her ears.

"Me?" he had roared, "take another wife after I've been wed to your sainted mother?"

She imagined he would debase himself to wheedling to change her mind, for he had grown accustomed to having her here these last many months. However, she made a decision, and when she made a decision, she was not easily swayed. As soon as Dan came again, she would return with him to Adair County.

Blessedly, there was a break in the weather. It was nearly spring. The sun had come out as if confirmation, raising her spirits, and she went about the house humming to herself. Marnie had not uttered a tune since she arrived, and Mae's face was filled with curiosity and suspicion.

Yet, Mae kept her opinions to herself. She had known Marnie practically all of her life and could have molded her in a different direction if Clay hadn't been so permissive. But in a way she had to admire the courage that had become such a part of who she was. Right in the middle of the Confederate army she had gone! In spite of her fear!

CHAPTER TWENTY-EIGHT

AFTER THE BATTLE of Mill Springs, some of the Union men returned to Clinton County to organize companies to combat the rebels that were rampant throughout the county. Clay Spencer was one of the first to join a company of what they once again called Home Guard. They were useful against minor groups of rebels and in obtaining and relaying information concerning enemy movements to the Federal forces across the river.

Dan Cable had never returned to Clay's home since the last of November, and it was nearly the first of April. Marnie's heart felt strangely lost and alone and she wondered why he never came back. She was tempted to ride to the Cable place and inquire if Dan had been there. In the end, she decided against it, for they wouldn't understand, and as a married woman, would perhaps question her motives. She was ready to return to Adair County, and at his absence, her hope of doing so grew dimmer and dimmer with each passing day.

Clay did hear some good news through the grapevine, though. Bob Witter had enlisted with the Sixth Confederate Cavalry. Upon hearing that, Marnie felt relieved somewhat, for in going about the county, she was fearful of coming upon him alone somewhere. And heedless to what Duke Morgan had ordered, she felt he would have done her harm if he could have done it circumspectly. Bob Witter was what someone would characterize as 'mean clear through' according to Clay.

Clay and Ed stopped sleeping at home at night, due to the rebel bands that roamed the county. It became a common occurrence that Union men were surprised in the night, and shot for the very fact they stood for the north. The Federals stayed north of the Cumberland and bushwackers and guerrillas created havoc throughout the county. But for the most part, the women were not harmed.

Loathe to be so far from the women, Clay refused to go to the valley, except for seeing after the stock. Instead, he and Ed made a double pen of fence rails, a quarter mile from the house in the edge of the north pasture. Stuffed with straw for warmth, they put clapboards over the pen and piled brush on until the pen was not visible. In this pen, they slept unless Federals were nearby. During the day they kept a watchful eye for any States Righters in the vicinity of the home.

It had showered a late snow for the season and quickly began to melt. Marnie was once again called to the Harmon house. Bessie's child had contracted diarrhea and a fever, according to Cary.

Marnie wiped her wet boots on the rug outside, and when entering the cabin, the smell was evident when she stepped through the door. She crossed to the cradle.

The baby lay listless. Not moving, not crying. Marnie's brows knit together in concern at the condition of the child.

"How long has the baby been sick?" she asked Bessie.

"Three days now."

Three days! A baby with diarrhea for three days!

"Why didn't you call me sooner?"

Bessie lowered her head and her voice was like a whisper and Marnie had to bend to hear her. "I was afraid, Mrs. Cross. I was afraid if Cary left, the horse would be stolen from her. And that's the only horse we've got."

A horse!

She could understand with all the horse stealing going on about losing the horse, but when your child is sick? Looking at Bessie's bowed head, she remembered Stephen was gone and Bessie was just a child herself, and compassion took the place of aggravation.

It would do no good to try boneset for the child, for it was unconscious and would not be able to swallow. And for one so young and with chronic diarrhea, the only thing to do now was wait…wait for death.

Marnie asked Cary for some snow. That would, at least, cool the fever a little. But it would not be long….

Bessie Harmon's baby died. Died before it had a chance to really live.

Evening was drawing on and Clay watched Marnie come up the drive. When he got her attention, he motioned her to the barn.

"Where have you been trotting off to now?" Clay asked, testily when she stepped down from her horse. "I declare, you're the only person in this county that can hold onto a horse when everyone else gets theirs' stolen. I suppose I've got to chalk that up to the doings of Duke Morgan. As bad as he is, I believe, girl, you've got that man bewitched."

"Please, Pa," she said wearily and stretched her back. "I've been to the Harmons and—"

"That Harmon bunch that are States Righters? You've been there consorting with them with all that's been going on?"

"Pa," she said quietly, "will you please listen to me?"

"Go ahead," he snorted. "But you'd better have a good explanation."

"Bessie's baby died. I couldn't save him."

Clay had no answer to that.

"I have a favor to ask of you, Pa."

"What is it?"

"I want you to make a casket to bury the child in."

Clay looked at her in disbelief.

"A casket? With all our soldiers being buried who knows where on battlefields, and you want me to make a box for sesech?"

Marnie stared at him, speechless. "Pa," she finally argued, "that child was not Confederate…nor was he Union. He was just a baby, Pa. Just a few months old. And you can't do a Christian deed by making something to lay him in for a final resting place?"

With that being said, she angrily turned on her heel and walked to the house.

Marnie rose early before daylight the next morning with the intention of riding to the Harmon place. The child needed to be buried and she had promised Bessie she would bring the casket and oversee the little funeral, such as it would be.

After a quick breakfast, she went to the barn to see what she could fashion out of some scrap wood her father had, and to her surprise, her horse was already hitched to a wagon. But it wasn't just that that drew her surprise. It was the fact that a proper burying box had been built and was already loaded onto the wagon, and she knew this was the work of her father.

Her father took a great chance working on it during the night, for that was especially the time when the raiders rode, and Ed must have stood guard while he worked. Her heart melted when she thought of what he had done. For as hard as he was against Southern sympathizers, he could still find some compassion for a helpless child. Perhaps he did it out of guilt and duty, but she knew his heart. She did not question whether his belief about the war was right or wrong, for she understood that freeing the slaves was a moral objective. She also understood that in this county it had become personal, old vendettas were finally given an opportunity to be carried out. And in spite of his ranting about Confederates, her father was a good Christian.

She drove the wagon out of the barn. And in the harsh early light, she smiled.

Marnie stood, spade in hand, beside the dirt she was soon to shovel back in place. Bessie and Cary stood behind her, trying to keep their eyes from the cavity in the ground that held the little boy. There had been no preacher and Marnie had read appropriate Scripture and prayed the appropriate prayer. Though the ground had thawed somewhat, it was still frozen and unforgiving, and though it was somewhat a shallow grave, instead of six feet deep, it still took Marnie most of the day to dig it. Filling in the grave, she then took the wagon to gather enough large stones to top the grave, and then, with Bessie and Cary, piled them on top.

There was no offer of payment, but then few had the price to pay these days. These hill people were a proud people, and often felt something, anything, be it a bit of corn or honey, should be paid. It was an embarrassment not to be able to offer anything. So often, she would have a cup of coffee, laced with cream and insist that was payment enough.

She had been gone all day and it was nearly dark.

Truly, she had never felt so tired, and flexing her muscles, envied the strength of a man. She would surely be sore tomorrow and looked forward to spending a day doing nothing but sitting in the sunshine on the porch.

As she drove in the drive, she was startled to see several saddle horses tied up out front of the house. Is the Home Guard having a meeting at this time of night? she thought. Surely not, when the rebels rode at night doing their worst. Had something happened while she was gone?

Once at the house, she jumped from the seat, and let the reins drop. The dogs rushed to meet her and she ignored their friendly greeting. Hurrying in, she saw men circled around something she could not see, and trying to understand what was happening, she quietly pushed her way through them.

There her father lay on the divan surrounded by several men in the Home Guard. "What happened?" she immediately asked, but they merely stood, hats in hand, heads bowed. She instantly crossed to him and after realizing he was dead, uttered in a voice choked with anger, “W—who did this?”

At no reply, her eyes flashing, she stood to her feet and looked at the men and again asked, “Who did this?” and had a hard time drawing an easy breath.

“Was it Duke Morgan? Tell me—was it Duke?”

One of the Home Guard, Matt Geron, spoke up, “No, Mrs. Cross. It wasn’t Duke. He’s off on a scout with General John Hunt Morgan. We found Clay on the road like this. Most probably shot by a bushwacker.”

Bushwacker! To be shot like this when her father had never bushwacked anyone in his life!

In her stunned silence, suddenly Mae appeared in the doorway of the kitchen. Crying, she said, “Clay was worried about you, Marnie. When you didn’t come home, he was afraid something had happened and went to look for you. I didn’t want him to go by himself, but he wouldn’t hear of it,” and wiping her eyes with her apron, turned back to the kitchen.

CHAPTER TWENTY-NINE

THE STILL HOUSE with the sense of death upon it pressed about her until she felt she could not bear it any longer and she arose quietly, and took sanctuary on the porch.

Everything was fresh and green, the sun was shining, the robins had appeared, searching the ground for worms, but she didn't see them. The birds were singing, but she didn't hear them.

The Home Guard had come and put Clay in his final resting place in the little burying ground beside her mother, behind the paling fence. No preacher was there to sermonize. In fact, no preacher was around anywhere these days. Neither was religion. Killing and looting prevalent, there was something wrong with this county. If it wasn't Confederate guerrillas raiding and killing Union supporters, then it was Union guerrillas against Southern sympathizers. All the same…all in the name of war. But should the Home Guard know her thoughts, she would be labeled "treasonous".

Mae and Ed did not intrude upon her, believing that she wished to be left alone. The house was quiet. Mae did not rattle the pans and Ed, becoming distant, had disappeared somewhere. But they did not understand. Added to her sense of loss at her father's death, remorse was awakened in her bosom as she looked upon his coffined face.

She had killed him. She had killed him just as surely as if it had been she, waiting beside the road…her finger that pulled the trigger. He did not like her going about the county as she did, and expressly said so many times. She had taken advantage of the fact that though he had begged her, he would not forbid her for he was so happy to have her home again. She had refused to listen to him, thinking she had immunity from any harm. Even going among the Confederate army had filled her with a sense of inordinate pride. She came through unscathed, and instead of giving thanks to God for her safe return, she gloried in her courage. She wondered if Mae and Ed thought the same of her.

Pride goeth before destruction, and a haughty spirit before a fall.

She could have taken more precautions, but didn't. She could have asked Ed to go with her so her father would not worry, but didn't. He had no involvement in the Home Guard and had no real worry about harm as long as he surrendered his horse, if approached. And even at that, he would have had some level of protection with her along.

Her father's love for her bade him to go look for her, and now he was dead because of her obstinacy and she would never look on his face again. She thought of her mother. So many years that she had been gone and only her portrait on the mantel precipitated a clear reminiscence of her in her mind. How long before her father's image would begin to fade? Even now, the features of the faces of Judah and Benjamin were dimming and a sense of fright was trying to capture her heart at the loss. And what of Grandfather and Grandmother Spencer? Their request in the letter that 'Clay come home for it had been so long since they had looked upon his face'. How would they react now, never to see him again, and how could she tell them it was her fault?

Marnie did not want to be alone. For a moment she thought about going into the kitchen and seeking comfort from Mae, but she hesitated. Mae, weeping since last night, would probably make matters worse for she had been a strong voice against her traispings about, even as a girl with Granny Forbes. And she could not bear to face any reprisals from her right now. Mae had been with Clay for so many years, he was like a son to her and Marnie sensed condemnation from her though she kept silent about it.

Marnie drew a deep sigh. If only Dan were with her, Dan could calm her fears. Since his disappearance several months ago, she had wondered about him. He seemed so preoccupied and unsettled at his last visit when she had gone into the Confederate camp. Was he wounded in battle as were so many she had been hearing of from the county? If he had only come months ago, she would have left with him. Clay would still be alive. She was brought up short at that thought. She struggled for a few moments and her sense of right and wrong won the battle. The truth stood out boldly and she cowered away from it. Her conscience would not allow her to excuse her behavior and lay it at Dan's doorstep. No…this was no other's doing, but her own.

She glanced at the barn. Her father took great pride in that structure. He had painted it just last year and repaired the corral. One of the finest around, never again would she see Clay Spencer riding proudly out of it on one of his magnificent horses.

A figure appeared on the drive, riding a bay mare, and, in fear, for an instant she thought the spirit of her father had returned to haunt her.

As the rider approached, her heart leaped with sudden recognition. It was Dan Cable! Gladness flooded her and she nearly jumped from her seat to race toward him, but something told her that Mae was looking out the window, and who knew where Ed might be, so she stayed still.

Dan reached the house, dismounted his horse and tied him to the rail. He stood at the bottom of the steps for a moment, one foot poised on the first step and looked at her briefly. Marnie half-rose, and when Dan ascended the rest, she took her seat again.

She had not cried since Clay's death, she had wanted to, but guilt had had her in its grip so strong.

Dan sat down in a chair beside her in silence, his eyes alertly searching her face, noting the white pallor of her skin.

"You came." She stated flatly, speaking from a deep well of rejection.

He nearly winced when she spoke those words. "Of course, I did," he said. I came straightaway once I heard." He paused when she refused to meet his eyes. "You needed me."

Needed him? Of course, she needed him, had for the last few months, but he hadn't come, hadn't taken her home.

Sudden tears filled her eyes, tears that had threatened but did not appear before this minute.

"He was bushwacked. Bushwacked, Dan! He didn't deserve that!"

He did not immediately answer. "We're at war, Marnie," he said at last in a slow voice.

"This isn't war," she argued his point of view. "It was pure and simple ambush!

"I know Pa was so outspoken about the Confederates, in fact about a lot of things," she continued, "but you know there's more to it than that, Dan. Some of these people in this county live by their own code, and when offended, look for a way to even the score, even if they have to do it in the name of war. They blame Pa for shooting Zane McKendrick for cattle rustling years ago, and that family has held a grudge against him ever since…with the exception of Kara, of course. But she is Judah's aunt and only married into them. Pa didn't kill him. Judah's father and others with him did. But they always believed that Pa was responsible for it was his cattle being rustled. And no matter that Zane was guilty, they hold to 'an eye for an eye'. I can't prove it, but reason makes me think it was one of them."

"Well, until you have proof, be careful," he quickly warned. "If you go around accusing people when you have no evidence, they are likely to come after *you*. And if they have compunction about killing a woman, they, nevertheless, wouldn't hesitate to harass you in other ways."

Marnie drew a long breath, and continued. "I don't know if you know it, but Judah's father went into hiding from a family that wanted revenge. He hid for twenty years before the last one caught up with him and Clell was forced to kill him in this county."

"I heard of it," he admitted.

"Is this the way it will be for all generations to come?" she asked in exasperation.

Dan was born and raised in this county and knew of what she had spoken, for feuds were not unheard of, and he had heard of the McKendrick—Spencer feud for years, though no overt action had ever been taken. It had all been talk…until now.

"I have no answer to that, Marnie," he said simply. "We live and answer for our own actions."

Our own actions. My actions.

At those words, her heart plummeted and she cast her eyes down. Her hands which had been animated with speech, were suddenly still in her lap.

Dan sensed some other matter was disturbing her. It was more than just losing her father.

"What's the matter, honey?" he said softly, and she was so upset that the endearment did not register with her.

She raised tormented eyes to his face. How could she explain to him what she was wrestling with—that it was all her fault? Would he think her a spoiled, wanton woman, reckless in her actions?

"Can't you tell me?" He covered her hand with his, gentle in his touch.

"Oh, Dan!" she finally cried. "Me—I'm the one to blame for Pa's death. It might as well have been me that pulled the trigger!"

"Tell me what you mean." His voice was calm and soothing.

Tears were streaming unheeded down her face now. "Pa didn't want me going about the county like I was, and I ignored, and…sometimes laughed at him. He worried so. I buried Bessie Harmon's baby and when I didn't come home, Pa came looking for me.

“You’re his daughter. It’s only normal he would search for you.”

She shook her head. “You don’t understand. I’ve been spoiled and selfish, going my own way, heedless to any danger. Even when going into the Confederate troops, I’ve been thinking since then that I’m so brave. Been downright proud of it, I have! You know what the Bible says about ‘lofty eyes’. ‘The lofty looks of man shall be humbled’. I haven’t thanked God that was He that was with me and kept me safe!”

He fumbled in his pocket for a handkerchief and handed it to her. “You might have gotten off-track a little there, but I don’t look at it quite that way,” he said with quiet insistence.

“You’ve always taken care of others…have since you were a girl. There are times you might have been a bit careless, but we’ve all been that way at some time or another.”

“But—” she floundered helplessly. “I could have listened to Pa.”

“You could have—if you’d been somebody else. You are you. You have a gifting that many others don’t have. You want to help others with what God has put in your life. It’s a part of you, in fact, it’s who you are. Your father loved you and wanted you to be what God created you to be. Even though he worried, Clay understood that and allowed you to be yourself. How many other women would have gone about the county, tending the sick, in spite of danger?”

He smiled a teasing smile. “You even agreed to work with me as a spy.”

Her face clouded and she sniffed as she shifted in the chair. “That’s only because you said you’d get Judith out of here if I did. Otherwise, I would not have done it.”

“See what I mean?” he said. “You weren’t thinking of yourself, but your daughter. Clay was a good man, Marnie, thinking of you, even as you put yourself in harms’ way thinking of Judith.”

She sat in silence for a few moments trying to digest what he had just said and the astonishing fact that he had been talking about God. The quiet confidence in his voice reassured her.

He was thinking his own thoughts as he stared at her face. He was hopelessly in love with her, and had deliberately stayed away from her these last few months—spending much time with the army, with the added fact that he no longer wanted to put her life in danger by being a spy.

He stood up suddenly, casting a long shadow.

"What do you want to do, Marnie, now that Clay is gone?"

She craned her neck and looked up into his eyes, relief and appreciation shining through her tears.

Rising from her chair, she put a hand on his sleeve. At her touch, she sensed some inner struggle within him as he seemed to pull back a mite. But as for herself, she felt safe…safe that he would take care of her.

"Take me home, Dan," a hint of pleading in her eyes and voice. "Take me home to Adair County."

And he thought: "If she had said, 'Take me to the moon', I would try."

CHAPTER THIRTY

THE TOWN OF COLUMBIA was a far cry from when she had left nearly a year ago. Marnie looked about in awe, twisting this way and that, at the tangle of wagons, buggies, and a sea of blue uniforms. Passing by the hospital, a small army milled about it. Businesses were brisk with the influx of new faces. A wagon train with supplies was just pulling into the town and caught the immediate attention of soldiers, the look of alertness on their lean faces, waiting for weapons, ammunition, and other supplies for disbursement throughout other counties to the army.

For the last year, she had been so engrossed in the misplaced civilities of Clinton County, that Marnie did not know since the fighting began, Columbia had been so transformed. The town, as she knew it, was gone and in its place, was busy as a beehive, changed into a rapidly growing city.

In spite of Marnie's pleading to go with her, Mae refused to accompany her to Adair County, and Ed Ferrill stayed with her to look after the ranch. Marnie supposed Clay had a will somewhere, but she was in such a hurry to leave, she didn't take time to look for it. Well, she determined, it would do no good at this point as all legal proceedings in Albany had practically come to a halt with Confederates in town most of the time.

Her mind was not on Clinton County as she ascended the steps to her house. She entered the home, walked slowly from room to room taking note of the furnishings. Nothing was moved, nothing had changed. Had she really expected it to this last year?

She entered into Judah's library where they had had many arguments about his enlistment. His desk was covered with a thick layer of dust. The room smelled musty and she opened the window for an airing. Like a schoolgirl, she leaned out the window and looked over the vast estate. Spring was in the air. Trees were leafing out, and the yellow jonquils in the yard were displaying the last of their showy blooms. Several small homes for families that worked on the estate stood empty.

Many men had enlisted and, with the exception of a few, their wives and children had returned to live with their families, and there were few children playing about. Wade Caulder was turning up the sod in the garden, preparing for seed to be planted in the ground. With a sigh, she realized it had never been this quiet before.

What will I do now? she thought. What was anyone doing these days?

There was nothing in the house to eat. She was hungry, she needed a bath, and she was tired. It had been a hard trip and as a breeze fluttered the dusty curtains, she went to sit in the chair. It was comfortable after sitting in the saddle for so long. Her eyes closed and she relaxed in the coziness of the chair. It felt good to sleep, to rest. Smiling and half asleep, her hands, that had held reins for so long, relaxed in her lap. She was not quite asleep, not quite awake and then she dozed.

A knock on the door sounded. She reluctantly heard it, struggled against coming fully awake, then settled back to dozing again. Louder this time, it sounded, and she reluctantly roused awake. The little rest had left her groggy. She got slowly out of the chair at the third knock and made her way sleepily to the front door.

Marnie gave a wide yawn as she placed her hand on the knob and shook the cobwebs out of her head. She opened it and….

Not believing who she saw in the doorway, she stood there for a bit, blinking repeatedly before she uttered, "Benjamin!" and threw herself into his arms.

Drawing him into the parlor, she bade him to sit while she did the same and feasted her eyes on him. It had been so long since she had last seen him. He was no longer the soft boy that left Clinton County. He was hard and lean and had a mustache. A quiet air of self-reliance was about him now, coupled with alertness.

They spoke of mundane topics for a few minutes, about home, the stock, crops, the fact that he had had the measles, and Wade Cauldron.

"How did you know I was home?"

"I saw you ride through Columbia and figured this was the first place you would come. How have you been, Mother? I saw a man with you, although I didn't get a good look at him."

"That was Dan Cable with me. He brought me home. He had to stop off in Columbia, but he'll be here later with some of my things."

"Cable?"

"Yes. He's from Clinton County and is here with the army."

"Oh, yes, I know him. I guess just about everybody does. Tough man and great in battle."

Uh-oh, he thought suddenly as she opened her mouth to speak. He had spoken the word 'battle' and that was enough opening for her to pour forth a tirade of questions that he was in no mood to answer.

"Why did you come back?" he interrupted. "I thought you wanted to stay with Grandfather."

She got up and paced the room, swift passion flushing her face. "I just had to." She turned to him. "Oh, Benjamin, something terrible has happened. Your grandfather is dead!" she cried in anguish.

"Grandfather Sam?" he asked in surprise.

"No. Not your great-grandfather. It's my father…Clay."

"Grandfather Clay?"

"Yes. He was bushwacked. I—I just couldn't stay there any longer."

"Bushwacked! But who—?"

"I don't know, but I've got my suspicions. I don't know how to tell Grandfather Sam and Grandmother Rachel. How can I face them with this kind of news?"

"I don't know, Mother. I suppose our commanding officers feel the same way when they have to write and tell someone their loved one is dead."

"Oh, Benjamin," she sat down, and in a swoop turned to him. "It's so awful down there right now. You know I sent Judith home, don't you?"

He nodded. "I know it's been pretty bad. Our Adair County Home Guard was sent there a few months ago. I've been there a few times with the army and we drove them out. Of course, that was only temporarily, for they always came back."

"You were in Clinton County," she said astounded, "and you didn't try to see me?"

"Frankly, Mother, I wasn't sure you wanted to see *me*."

"Not want to see you? Oh, Benjamin, I would have fallen on my knees and thanked God to see you again."

"Well…I know how you feel about Father. Mother…can't you make peace with him leaving? You know he is a peaceable man and felt if there was any other choice, he would have stayed."

She didn't answer that question, and instead asked, "Where is your father? Is he in Columbia?"

"In and out."

"And you—are you with him?"

"Yes, at times."

"Are you in battles most of the time?"

Seeming disinclined to talk, Benjamin put his head down, and shrugged his shoulders. "We mostly focus on disrupting Confederate supply lines and gathering intelligence, Mother. There are a few skirmishes, though," he confessed.

"Were you at the Battle of Mill Springs?"

She was probing too much and he got quickly to his feet. He did not want to talk about battles and skirmishes. This was home, and he wanted to feel he could leave all that outside the door. He wanted to smell home cooking, lay down on a soft bed where rain or sleet or snow did not trespass.

"I can't stay, Mother," he said, a touch of exasperation in his voice. "I've got to get back."

"But—but you just got here!" she cried.

Benjamin turned to leave and she crossed to where he stood and laid her hand on his arm.

A cold little fear struck her heart. Would she ever see her son again? Were these few precious minutes she spent with him all she would ever have?

"Promise me—promise me," she said, a little desperately, "Promise me, you'll come see me again."

From what he had witnessed at Mill Springs, he wasn't making any promises he could not keep.

"When I can," he reluctantly answered.

And watching him step into the saddle and ride away, tears stung her eyes, and dashing a hand across her eyes, Marnie thought, "I'm driving him away. I only try to draw him close, but I'm driving him away."

Then she remembered something. She had forgotten to ask about Seth McCord.

CHAPTER THIRTY-ONE

DAN ARRIVED with, not only the rest of her belongings, but enough food to last her a few days. He carried in wood to put in the wood box, and then started the wood cooking stove for her. Marnie made coffee, fried corn cakes to go with the ham, and told him she'd had a talk with Wade Caulder. He informed her that Zane Banyon had sold several head of cattle to the army. And when she asked him about the money, he did not know where it was and she determined it was nothing but thievery.

She examined the cutlery drawer. "Well at least he didn't get around to taking the silver," she threw over her shoulder to Dan as she extracted the cutlery from the drawer to set with table with.

As he watched her work, he made her feel mixed-up. Usually a talkative person, he was unusually quiet tonight. Whatever was he thinking? Was he so overwhelmed by this house? She noticed his continued attention to its furnishings. It was a fine home, a home that would rival those on the battery in Charleston. It was a grand home, indeed, for Jake Templeton had built it, and Jake had never done anything on a small scale.

She reached for the pot to pour coffee, and without thinking, gripped the handle barehanded. Crying out, she let go, the pot banging down on the stove and that hand was held in the other.

Dan leaped from the chair and wanted to examine her hand.

Instead, she said, "Get my medicine bag in the parlor, please."

Retrieving her bag, he opened it and brought out bandages and healing salve. She nearly winced as he applied the salve. "It's not so bad, really," she protested. "I've seen worse. And, being in battle, I'd say you've seem much worse."

"Hush," he said, and gave her a crooked smile as he bandaged her hand. "Don't you know I've wanted to hold your hand for a long time?"

She was taken off guard and grew still. Was he teasing her, trying to take her mind off the burn? His gentleness with her belied his military prowess. He was so close he could lower his face into her hair and breathe in the scent of freshly washed hair if he wanted to. She felt herself go hot and cold all over and fixed her eyes on the floor. She tried to think of anything but the nearness of him. The floor was dusty and needed a good scrubbing, and she made a mental list of the things to do…anything to take her mind off him. Could he see what she was trying to hide? Though she had fought it, and would continue to do so, he'd become embedded in her heart in ways she couldn't explain.

Putting the salve back in the bag, he set it on the counter and took a seat across the table from her.

She looked at the ham on her plate and reached for her knife and fork. Without speaking, he leaned across the table and cut the meat for her.

They said little during supper, and when it was over, she poured water into the pan to do the dishes. Over her protests, Dan made her go into the parlor and rest while he did them, explaining that he was used to doing for himself.

Cleaning the dishes, Dan did some soul-searching. He had been with her for two days and two nights. Two days of longing and loving, and with his hands in the suds, came to a decision. She was Judah's wife and, as such, he must stay away from her. He didn't like having a guilty conscience. It clouded his thinking. And regardless of what trouble lay between Judah and Marnie, he would not take advantage of their separation, and he would not taint her reputation by being a regular visitor to *The Crossing*.

He was in a sulky mood when he joined her in the parlor, refusing to look at her. He sat on a Windsor chair, his tall body dwarfing the furniture. Repressing a smile, Marnie thought Dan Cable was not a man to feel at home with such furnishings and wondered how his home was furnished. Surely, something more primitive as skin covered over-stuffed chairs.

She sat quietly in the rocking chair, watching his face for some sign of what was on his mind. Whatever it was, she wasn't in the frame of mind for any more bad news. He had been so kind in tending to her needs this evening, it made her feel—she searched for the proper word, but could only think of "Loved".

He sat quietly, looking at his hands, his eyes avoiding her. She had never seen him so ill at ease before. The silence was awkward between them, and she was clueless as how to break the quiet as she searched her mind for some topic of conversation.

"I've—I've something to tell you," he began hesitantly.

Suddenly, fear that normally lay just barely surface, emerged. Whenever anyone prefaced a sentence in that way, it was usually bad news.

"Oh, no!" cried Marnie from the bottom of her heart and stopped rocking. "Has something happened to Judah?"

At Judah's name, Dan turned and looked at her, his eyes unfathomable. He looked at her face. She loved her husband, that fact was unmistakable by her anguished look.

"No," he said bluntly.

Her head fell forward and her shoulders slumped in relief, and she started her rocker again.

They were silent a while longer while he tried to gather his courage.

"Maybe it would be better if I did not see you anymore," he said abruptly, keeping his eyes averted.

She stopped rocking suddenly and her eyes grew big as saucers.

Not see me anymore?

Marnie's heart failed a beat when those words came again like an ocean wave in her mind, and her thoughts became vocal when she lifted her head and cried heatedly, "Why will you not see me anymore? What have I done?"

Dan gave her that look again.

"You're a mighty taking person, Marnie," said Dan candidly.

"Mighty taking? What are you talking about, Dan Cable?" she asked as her voice began to rise. "What's that got to do with anything?"

"I—I just can't explain it, Marnie," He threw his hands wide. "It's just something I must do."

Must do? After all we've been through together and now he says….

Her thoughts broke off and she questioned forlornly, "Is it—is it because I'm no further use to you as a spy?"

He swung around in a flash and looked at her with an intensity that frightened her.

"A spy?" he said with swift violence, and there was the sheen of pain in his eyes. "That's what you think? No," he shook his head, "that's not it. I shouldn't have asked that of you in the first place," he said with self-condemnation. "I put your life in jeopardy."

"Well—then—what is it?" she asked in confusion.

Dan's voice changed to gentleness.

He smiled a brief smile that never reached his eyes. "Are you so blind, that you can't see, Marnie?" His voice spoke of an ache within him.

He turned away and drew a deep breath. "If I keep seeing you, I'm lost."

I'm lost?

Not realizing she was holding her breath, she had no answer and the only sound was a ticking of the mantel clock. Tick, tick, tick.

Slowly he turned back to her. His eyes were like wells of deep water, reflecting his love and longing for her.

"I'm in love with you," he wanted to admit. "That's the simple truth of it."

But he couldn't.

Still—a man needed somebody to think about....

Marnie sat in stunned silence after Dan was gone. She could not even pass on the porch to say good-bye to him when he left. As evening drew on, and the house darkened, she still sat and repeatedly rehearsed their conversation.

"Am I so blind that I can't see?" she asked herself aloud. "What did he mean?"

She considered her situation. Grandmother Spencer wanted to keep Judith near her at *North Star*. Benjamin and Judah were gone. Her father was gone. Now Dan Cable was gone..."never to return," he said.

Through the window, in the faint light of the rising moon, *The Crossing* stretched before her, the fields, the stock, the gardens, and most workers gone. Until this moment she had not realized how much she had counted on Judah to take command, to tell her what she must do.

She was alone, and, for the first time since Judah enlisted...felt lonesome.

CHAPTER THIRTY-TWO

On Mat 20, 1862 President Lincoln signed the Homestead Act, effective January 1, 1863, giving 160 acres of western public land to any person, provided that the person settled on the land for five years and then paid a nominal fee. If settlers wished to acquire title earlier, they could do so after six months at $1.25 an acre.

MARNIE HAD RETURNED to *The Crossing,* yet spent considerable time at the Stone Valley Springs Hotel.

The cool rains of April passed into the warmer green of May weather. The weeks were packed with work at, not only the hotel, but at home, too.

Marnie had followed her uncle, Dr. Adam McClelland about the first day as he informed her of the condition of the patients. Some had died, he said, with gangrene and blood poisoning which had set in before they could reach Columbia and a doctor. Some had developed pneumonia and others lay recuperating from dismembered limbs.

Some neighboring women were writing letters for the soldiers who were illiterate, and bandage rolling was an ongoing undertaking in what was once a millinery shop at the hotel.

The mineral water there was beneficial to the soldiers, as long as they did not drink too much at a time, and that was not a benefit the hospital in Columbia offered.

Though it had been months since the battle of Mill Springs, the hotel still had many convalescing men, and Wayside hospitals had been established by the local women of Adair County to accommodate the flow of the wounded that came in at various times.

It was the end of May, and after a busy morning, Marnie and Cole were sitting on the back porch of the hotel, drinking coffee.

"Well, what do you think of the Homestead Act signed by President Lincoln?" asked Cole, holding an open newspaper before him.

"Frankly, Cole, I don't know what you're talking about," murmured Marnie, clearly disinterested. It had been a busy morning, and she had assisted Adam, performing three surgeries, and she was tired from standing on her feet all morning. An outbreak of measles was ravaging the soldiers, and some of the nurses contracted it, too, leaving them shorthanded. And every lady who nursed at the hospitals brought home baskets of bloody strips to be washed and ironed and returned for use on other patients.

She was considering going home for the day and, perhaps, a few days. There was so much work to do at *The Crossing*. A few more head of stock had disappeared, and she was puzzled by it.

"The Homestead Act," he proceeded to answer, "states the Federal government is giving away 160 acres of public land to anyone that will settle in the west."

"Where in the west," she asked, interest piquing, "are they talking about?"

He bent his head back to the newspaper. "It seems it is Indian Territory, Nebraska, Kansas, and the Dakotas. In other words, land west of the Mississippi River."

"160 acres, you say?" she asked.

"Yes. It's right here in black and white."

She reached for the newspaper with, "Let me see," and scanned the article.

"Cole," she asked in thought, laying the paper down, "do you suppose people from around here have the notion about going?"

He nodded his head. "When they get wind of this, some will."

"What makes you think so?"

"They want to get away from war. However, they can't take advantage of the offer until the 1st of January. But that doesn't mean they won't start heading out that way now."

"But won't some be trading one war for another?"

Cole looked puzzled.

"You know, trading the War Of The Rebellion with war with the Indians?"

"I doubt that some will be thinking about it that way."

And she was thinking: "If it were not for this load I'm carrying, I'd be tempted to join them."

And when Judah came home—if he did come home…No, she would not think of that now.

"Wade Caulder is either utterly stupid or the most insipid person I've ever met," thought Marnie after she left him at the stables. His response to her questions, were either, "Yep," or "Nope," or a shrug of the shoulders as she talked to him, and she had left with more questions than answers.

Wade had stood, his back to her, working on a harness when she entered the stables. He did not turn around when she asked him questions, and worked the harness in his hands as though she had not come in at all.

Her stock was slowly diminishing, even her hogs and chickens, and when she asked him if it was the work of coyotes, his response was a mere shrug of the shoulders, and she thought any foreman worth his salt would investigate the situation.

"I'd fire him in a heartbeat," she fumed, as she stomped out of the stables, "if I thought there was someone else I could get."

She walked by the gardens. They were sadly neglected with weeds taking over their tender shoots. She would have to hoe them herself or there will end up being no gardens, and thought, with frustration that the estate was falling into ruin. Hotel or no hotel, she simply had to stay home for a while and see about the estate. Perhaps she would find answers to her vanishing stock.

Approaching Tess Banyon's home, she decided to stop. She had not been there in many days. Knocking on the door, she heard: "Come in," and opened the door and stepped into the parlor.

"Marnie!" Tess exclaimed, motioning for Marnie to sit. "What a surprise. I haven't seen much of you lately."

"Well…yes, I've been very busy with the soldiers and all.

"What news of Zane?" Marnie continued.

"I haven't heard anything lately." Her face held a trace of apprehension. "He was here a couple of months ago, though."

I wonder if he sold stock to the army when he was here, Marnie wondered.

"I've been meaning to ask you, Marnie," Tess ventured with a tentative smile. "Do you mind if I share my meals with you? I mean, you being so busy and all, not having time to cook, and being up there in that big house by yourself."

She looked at Tess. There was a certain quietness of manner about her that Marnie had always been drawn to.

"Mind? Of course not. Why would you ask such a thing?"

Tess hesitated, her face strained. "Uh—you've been kind of distant since you came back. I just wondered if something is wrong."

Marnie's reserve left her. She had known Tess most of her life. When Tess became pregnant out of wedlock with Zane by cattle rustler, Zane McKendrick years ago, it was Judah who allowed her to come to *The Crossing* to have her child, and gave her a place to live. And for that, Tess was grateful and had been a faithful friend all these years. Though people didn't know about the untimely birth, Tess always guarded her secret with ferocity. Zane's reputation must be preserved at all costs.

How could she tell Tess her suspicions about Zane? Especially, as he was not here to answer for himself.

Marnie smiled and reached over for Tess' hand.

"Think nothing of it, Tess. I just have a lot of responsibility right now. I do have a request to make of you, though. Help me gather the few folk here to tend to the gardens. If we're going to have any decent crops at all, I'll need all the help I can get."

Leaving Tess, Marnie passed by the estate's church. Climbing the steps, she opened the door and looked around. She had been so busy it had been a while since she had prayed in a church. Thank goodness they still had a preacher. Reverend Harry Miles had not lost his head and rushed off to war, and the fact that he was not a young man was a deciding factor in keeping him here. And a fine work he was doing, too, visiting the soldiers at the hotel.

Yet, still, there was a fervor pulsating throughout the county about the war, and neither young nor old were exempt from its enthusiasm. And families of wounded men in the hospital crowded Columbia insisting on being near them as they recuperated.

The Reverend was not here right now, but she didn't need a preacher to pray. Making her way to the altar, she knelt down. She prayed. She prayed for Judah and Benjamin. She prayed for Seth McCord and Dan Cable. She prayed for the war to end, but there were no answers.

What was it the Bible said? *We walk by faith, and not by sight.* Truly, she needed all the faith she could muster right now.

CHAPTER THIRTY-THREE

SPRING PASSED into summer, and as summer crept toward fall, on October 7th a battle was begun at Perryville, Kentucky that brought still more wounded into Columbia.

Receiving the news and hurriedly arriving at the hotel, Marnie halted, appalled at what she saw, and instinctively took a step back. In all her years in the medical field had she ever encountered anything of this magnitude.

Amid the tangle of ambulances and covered ordnance wagons carrying the wounded, men lay prostate on the ground, crying out "Water." Stretcher bearers lifted the moaning wounded, their wounds unbandaged, blood drying, faces black from powder stain.

Marnie pushed her way between the litter bearers. Inside, dining tables were positioned in the great foyer, and ambulance men hurried here and there transporting the wounded from vehicles to tables. Women moved among them, cleaning wounds, attempting to stop the flow of blood with bandages, but no sooner were they applied, they were red again.

Among the group, Adam McClelland frantically wielded his knife, his shirt and trousers already red with blood. His face had the look of a man overwhelmed by the enormity of the task at hand.

She hurried to him, and for a brief moment he looked at her through eyes that barely took notice of her.

"Thank God, you're here. Come around on the other side," he said a little roughly. "You can assist."

For two days Marnie stayed at the hotel with Adam and Cole, tending to the wounded. She no longer took note of the faces of those they performed surgery on, concentrated only their wounds, unending wounds. With only snatches of time to eat and sleep, she was tired, as were all the other workers.

Untying the scarf on her head, she was ready to leave for *The Crossing*, her shawl hiding some of the dress stained with blood. Wearily, she thought the dress was beyond redemption and could not be worn again.

Heading for the door, she heard: "Miss Cross!"

Turning toward the voice, she saw with surprise it was none other than Zane Banyon.

"Miss Cross!" he cried again.

She crossed the floor to him, wending her way between patients.

"Miss Cross," he said, a smile capturing his face. In spite of being wounded, he was still a captivating young man.

"Why, Zane," she said in surprise, laying a hand on his arm. "I didn't know you were here. Are you all right?"

"Yes'm," he answered. "Just a hip wound, but I'll be as right as rain. You and Adam operated on me, but I guess you didn't take much notice, as busy as you were."

"I didn't know you were in the Battle of Perryville."

"Yes, ma'am. And what a battle it was! Worst one I've been in!" he exclaimed.

A sudden thought occurred to her.

"Zane, was Judah or Benjamin at Perryville?"

His brow furrowed in thought. "What outfit are they with?"

"Wolford's cavalry."

He shook his head. "I don't think so, ma'am. But I don't rightly know."

Zane rose up on one elbow. "Would you get word to my mother? Tell her I am all right and am here."

"I will, Zane. I'm heading home now."

"Thank you, ma'am. Thank you," he said gratefully, and lay back down.

Marnie arrived home to find Tess waiting for her.

"I've been so worried about you, Marnie," she said as Marnie hung her shawl on the hall tree. "I've heard there was a big battle and the town is in an uproar with all the wounded coming in. I actually thought about riding over to offer my help, but I've never done any nursing before and didn't know if I would be a help or hindrance."

Marnie sank into a chair and put her head in her hands. "I wouldn't have noticed that you were there, even if you had come. So many surgeries. I've never seen the like of it before and hope to never see anything like it again."

She lifted her head and looked at Tess. "Oh, I have some news for you. Zane is at the hotel. He was in the fight."

Tess' hand came to her mouth in fright.

Marnie smiled. "Don't be alarmed," she said, averting a crying episode she saw coming. "He's all right. Just a hip wound. He wanted you to know, and I believe he'd like to see you."

"Oh, I will. I will. I'll go tomorrow straightaway."

Tess turned to prepare the meal, then on second thought, turned back again.

"I've got some news of my own to tell you."

"Yes?"

"Wade Caulder is gone. He said to tell you that he's heading out west to claim some land for himself." She drew her brow in a frown. "I believe he called it something like 'Homestead Act', whatever that is."

Gone? Leaving me in the lurch like this? None of it makes sense, she thought. As poor spirited as he's been, I never thought he'd have the gumption to strike out on his own.

Then a thought occurred to her.

"Tess. Have you ever seen Wade drive any stock off the place?"

"Well, yes, several times," she admitted. "I just supposed he was helping the army out."

He was, indeed, and helping himself in the process. Liar, he was, blaming Zane Banyon. Wade, a thief, took off with the money...her money.

CHAPTER THIRTY-FOUR

1863

IT WAS CLOSE TO CHRISTMAS and where, Marnie wondered, had 1862 and most of 1863 gone? To find her answer, she had only to take stock of the records at Stone Valley Springs Hotel. Sitting in the office, books opened before her, she drew her finger down the pages of those who had been treated and stayed for rehabilitation during Mill Springs Battle of 1861 and the Perryville Battle of 1862, and now it was the last of 1863 and the last of them were being released. Barring any major battle, the hospital and Wayside Stations could take care of any wounded coming in.

There was no news from Judah. Benjamin, she had thankfully seen a handful of times.

Oh, Lord, wherever they are, please let no harm come to them.

Tired, she put her hand on the back of her neck, and craned it back in stretching.

A knock sounded on the door, and as it opened, Cole peered around it.

Taken off guard, she felt a shock as she looked into the telling image of her father and tears came into her eyes. Would she never get used to seeing her father's twin without thinking of him lying behind the paling fence in Clinton County? The same dark hair, streaked with gray now, dark eyes, and a mouth that held a perpetual sliver of a smile as though he were about to play some kind of joke.

She tamped down her feelings and asked Cole to come in.

"What are you up to, Marnie?" he asked, looking at the ledgers before her.

"I'm thinking that perhaps we should close the hotel, Cole. The last of the soldiers will be leaving here, and it seems pointless to stay open any longer."

"I suppose so," he said. "But we could open it as a hotel again and take in patrons."

"Who would come?" she asked. "And remember, Duke Morgan and his cohorts came into Columbia in October when most our troops were gone. They nearly wiped out every store in town. People are terrified another raid will come. And, pray tell, what would we feed them? There wasn't enough help to raise many crops at *The Crossing*, Cole. Pretty much what we've had has been to feed the soldiers. We were never open for the winter season, anyway."

"That may be, but these are different times. We don't have to have all the trappings we had before the war such as dances and all, just scale things down a bit.

"To tell you the truth," he continued, a thoughtful look on his face, "I don't believe a few dances would be a bad idea, anyway. There's not much going on in the way of entertainment, and I think a bit of frivolity might take folks' minds off their troubles. We could even advertise potluck and let people bring in their own dishes or just offer something to drink."

"But most of the men are gone to war!" she declared. "And many women are in mourning."

"They may be in mourning, all right," he said, his dark eyes lighting up, "but if I were a betting man, I'd lay you two to one the girls won't be."

At her forthcoming objections, he continued, "Oh, I know there are still some men around that have convalesced, but won't be returning to service, either for a while or not at all, and there are plenty of girls that would jump at the opportunity to, shall we say, 'land a husband'?" A grin covered his face. "And who knows? There may be quite a few soldiers from Columbia that would attend."

"Looking for a wife for yourself, are you, Cole?" she gently teased.

"Now, Marnie, you know me," he gently chided. "I'm a confirmed bachelor."

Marnie's mind turned back in memory to the balls and dances held not so long ago. It seemed ages since she'd heard music and danced with Judah. Would she ever do so again?

"How would we advertise?"

"I'll take care of that," he told her. "I'll go to town and run off a few bills and post them around town."

Taking the calendar from the desk, Cole laid it in front of her on top of the ledgers. "Now…pick a date."

Marnie climbed the wide stairs and entered the door of the Grand Ballroom. It had been nearly three years since she had been in this room, and Cole outdid himself, preparing arrangements displayed throughout the room.

The chandeliers, dark during the days of war, were now lit with hundreds of prisms reflecting rays from the hundreds of candles that they bore. A table laden with various pies and punch stood in a corner of the hall.

Suddenly the ballroom burst into life. If was full of girls, girls from the county, as well as out of town. There were many uniforms in the crowd. Many were not as resplendent as the beginning of the war, but in the eyes of the young ladies who had been deprived of male companionship, resplendent just the same. Men recently released from the hospital had come, some with their arms in slings, some with head bandages, and some on crutches, and she speculated out of the couples present, at least a half dozen marriages would take place in the near future.

Tess arrived on the arm of her son Zane. The bullet to his hip had left him with a permanent limp. However his defect had no effect on his personality for he was still able to charm the birds out of the trees, and Marnie thought Judith would have a difficult time keeping him to herself tonight.

A platform was made for the musicians and they were preparing to play. Where did Cole find so many musicians?

The orchestra burst into "When Johnny Comes Marching Home", and the already excited crowd took up the song.

When Johnny comes marching home again,
Hurrah, hurrah!
We'll give him a hearty welcome then,
Hurrah, hurrah!
The men will cheer, the boys will shout,
The ladies, they will all turn out,
And we'll all feel gay,
When Johnny comes marching home.

Voices swelled with the next four verses, and when the band switched to a waltz, the dance floor became crowded with couples.

"A fine turnout, isn't it?" Tess reflectively told Marnie. She had not been to a dance since she was a girl, and the sight of dancing couples made her wistful for what she had missed in life.

Marnie smiled a slight smile. All these many years Tess had devoted herself to her son. She had never considered that Tess might be lonely, and now she saw Tess in a new light, for she was lonely herself.

"Would you like to dance with someone, Tess?"

Tess immediately drew back. "Oh, Marnie!" she exclaimed in self-debasement. "It's been so many years. I'm not sure if I remember how." Looking around the room, she said, "Besides, who would want to dance with *me*?"

Marnie laughed. "Who? Why, there's any number of men that would love to dance with you, Tess. Your problem is you shut the door in the face of any man before he has a chance to knock on the door."

And before the words were completely out of her mouth, Harold Kessler was making his way to them.

Harold asked Tess to dance, and as Tess looked towards Marnie for approval, he laid a hand on her arm and whisked her away.

Marnie watched them dance and thought they made a good couple. Harold was a widower with two sons fighting for the Union. Who knows? Perhaps, Tess was dancing with her future husband. Cole had said the girls were looking for husbands, but he wasn't surely thinking of people like Harold and Tess, and Marnie held back a chuckle.

The evening wore on and Judith was able to ward off any ladies claiming dances with Zane. My! How the war had changed the behavior of some of the girls, a bold lot they were becoming! Marnie supposed the lack of eligible bachelors was fostering desperation in some.

Marnie started to the refreshment table for a glass of punch, and halted in mid-stride. There, standing in the door was Dan Cable in uniform.

How long since she last saw him! It had been a year and a half since he left, and he had said he would not return.

As in a trance, she watched him approach her and, reaching her, said nothing, but hungrily took in the sight of her face.

Without a word, he indicated the dance floor, and took her hand and drew her onto it as though time had not passed between them, and she did not resist.

A couple of times around the floor, and she suddenly came to herself. She gave him sharp attention, seeming to measure and gauge him in one glance. He had not changed much, except the look of alertness about him was more so.

She tossed in her head for some topic of conversation. Where had he been? Had he been in any battles?—but she had no claim on him, had no right to even consider a claim, and could think of nothing to say.

Reaching deep in thought for some way to open the conversation, she said, "You dance very well, Dan."

He drew back a little from her, and looking into her face, smiled and explained. "I'm dancing with you, aren't I?"

A sudden spark of anger flared in her. "Where have you been?" she demanded, trying to shake her hand loose from his hand. "You've been gone for well over a year and have sent no word.

Just like Judah, she thought.

"And you just stroll in here," she continued, "like—like—"

"Stop—stop," he begged with a grin.

"Did you miss me?" he asked, a thread of hopefulness in his words, and held her hand tighter.

"Of course, I have," she finally answered tartly. "You're my friend. So many I know are dead or injured."

"Well, as you can see, I'm not dead. And I'm not injured."

"Don't be presumptuous."

Cole was looking at Marnie and Dan through questioning eyes, and Marnie, seeing his disapproval, said, "I think we should sit down now. People are beginning to stare."

It was the first time he had held her like this and he liked the feel of her in his arms.

"You aren't committing any crime, are you?" he asked. "They're starting a waltz again. Let's dance."

"No, please, I beg you," she pleaded, pulling against him. "Let me go."

Dan's eyes swept the crowd with a practiced eye, and, with disappointment, relinquished his hold.

With a sweep of his hand, he said, "Lead the way."

She took a seat in a bower of greenery, and reluctantly indicated he should sit also.

Cole made his way to them, a protective look on his face. Who was this man that Marnie was so intimate with?

Marnie stood up quickly as Cole reached them. Dan did likewise, but did so as an afterthought.

"Cole," said Marnie, "I'd like to introduce you to Dan Cable. I met Dan in Clinton County and he escorted me here. Dan…my brother Cole."

Marnie heard her name called, and craning her neck to see who the caller was, Cole answered with, "Over here."

A dispatcher from Columbia had an envelope in his hand.

"This is for you, ma'am," he said.

For me? Oh, no!

Cole dismissed the dispatcher, and Marnie held the envelope in her hand, looking at it, heart racing in fear.

Cole took it from her and, opening the envelope, took out the message and took note it was from Colonel Frank Wolford. Reading it silently, he then looked at Marnie and in his eyes she saw a soberness that was uncommon for him.

"Regret to inform you," he read slowly aloud, and then cleared his throat. "Regret to inform you Doctor Judah Cross missing in action in Knoxville. Believed captured. Will keep you informed."

And with that said, Marnie fainted.

CHAPTER THIRTY-FIVE

IT WAS A frightening trip home, with Cole driving Marnie in the buggy and Dan following on horseback. She was wordless and stunned, and slumped in the corner of the buggy.

He was dead, she was sure of it, in some unknown grave as so many others were. It was her fault. She had treated him terribly, punishing him for deserting her, and now God had punished her by killing him.

Even when Cole and Dan escorted her into the house, she refused to speak of the telegram. It was as though her thoughts would come to fruition and she would finally hear the news of his death. Cole helped her to bed, and once there, she tried to pray. But the words would not come. There only fell on her a dreadful fear that Judah would never be back home again. She got up and reaching for her Bible atop the dresser, looked at the image of herself in the mirror above it. It was with surprise that she noted she had not changed. The whole world had changed, yet she was still looked the same, except her face was motionless and like stone. She reached for her Bible but could not open it. There was no comfort from God for she could not voice the entreaty for it.

She was so tired. Tired of thinking, tired of fighting, tired of living. She made her way back to a tearless bed, and pulling the coverlet over her, slept a dreamless sleep.

Colonel Wolford and his men returned to Columbia, and, in February 1864, finally received information of the whereabouts of Judah Cross. On numerous occasions Marnie had been to his office seeking information and late in February, Colonel Wolford told her the news she had been waiting for.

"Andersonville?" she repeated, parrot-like.

"Yes, ma'am," nodded Colonel Wolford. "A new prison in Georgia the Confederates opened up this month."

"Oh, Colonel, is there some way—Can't you somehow have him exchanged?" cried Marnie.

"I'm afraid not, ma'am," the stately colonel told her regretfully. "President Lincoln has halted all prisoner exchanges. But I must tell you, madam, your husband was an exceptional soldier under my command, and should I hear any further news, I will send word to you right away."

"Yes, yes," she murmured as she began to turn away.

"Thank you, Colonel, and good day to you, sir," and she stumbled her way out of the door.

"Have you heard the news?" Cole asked Marnie when she walked through the door of the hotel.

"What news, Cole?"

"Colonel Wolford has been arrested!"

"Arrested? For what?"

"It seems he disagrees with the President's policy of freeing the slaves and enrolling them as Federal soldiers and is making speeches against him. That naturally is a violation of the Fifth Article of War.

Marnie had no idea what he meant and so asked him.

"It means," he explained patiently, "that any officer who speaks disrespectfully of the President shall be court-martialed and dismissed from service! But Wolford immediately reported to General Schofield at Knoxville, and it seems he's merely being dismissed from service with no court-martial."

Dismissed! This is the middle of March! she thought. That kindly man that showed me such concern about Judah's capture and imprisonment! Who will I turn to now for any news?

Dan Cable was in Adair County at times in the next few months, and he never failed to procure leave often enough to see Marnie, even if it was for an afternoon. Marnie wanted, at times, to ask him about his statement that 'he would never return', but refrained. He was her last link with news about Clinton County, especially when he did finally confide to her that most of his time away was spent on scouting trips, ousting the rebels from Clinton County. The elusive Duke Morgan somehow always escaped, he told her.

Reports began to circulate about the conditions of Andersonville Prison. President Lincoln allowed no exchanges, and the Confederates barely had enough to feed themselves, much less the prisoners. As a result, many of the Union prisoners were dying for lack of food and disease.

Dan had leave for a few hours one afternoon in September, and sitting at Marnie's kitchen table drinking coffee, she questioned him about the rumors she had been hearing.

"I'm not sure you really want to know all the details, Marnie," he said, a frown on his face. "Can't we talk about something else?"

"No," she stated emphatically. "I believe you have heard much more than I have, and I want to know what kind of trouble Judah is in."

He pursed his lips together as he looked at her in thought. He was never one to carry on about swooning women. However, she was not such a one, and was, in fact, one of the strongest women that he knew.

"It's not pretty what I've heard."

"Go on," she insisted. "I want to know."

He shook his head. "It's like you've heard. The prisoners don't have much to eat and they're dying like flies, sometimes a hundred a day. They have no medicine for diseases, and I don't think it would do much good anyway. I've heard they're turning into figures of skeletons, so deprived of food, they are."

"Are you saying Judah may die in that place?"

He drew a deep breath. "I don't know, Marnie. I'm not God. You've got to understand, the South is starving as a whole. Their harbors have been bottled up so they can't receive goods. They don't have enough food to feed their own, so naturally they will consider the welfare of the prisoners last," he said bluntly.

"And to be perfectly frank, Marnie, all they're getting to eat is fat pork and dried peas and very little of that."

All they're getting to eat! And here we sit feasting on pie and coffee!

She sat there looking lonely, beautiful, and sad.

"He told me he would come back, Dan," she said quietly. "He promised me."

Dan hesitated. "They all say that, Marnie."

"He meant it, Dan," she insisted.

Dan looked at her carefully. "They all do."

When Marnie was seeing Dan to the door, she asked anxiously: "Dan," she began, "have you heard anything about Benjamin?"

"He's safe," replied Dan, his teeth showing beneath his newly grown mustache.

When he left that day, he was tempted to stay away from her…until he later heard the news….

"He's dead, Mother. Father is dead. He died in Andersonville Prison."

Benjamin dropped his hand, clutching the telegram in his fist that she refused to take.

When he had spoken those words, tears came into her eyes. No sobbing, just the welling of tears as her shoulders slumped in resignation.

She had known this. She had felt it from the moment she saw the paper in the Benjamin's hand. Knew it when he rode up the drive. Knew it when Judah enlisted.

Now she waited, but she felt nothing. There was nothing to feel. Later, she knew she would. For months now, Judah had seemed like somebody who had never really been. Like someone who had entered her life and left no evidence of being there, but for her children. There was nothing to think of now…nothing to wait for. She never really expected him to come back and the news was only a confirmation of what she had felt and feared all along.

"I wanted to come last night and tell you."

Marnie did not open her arms for him to embrace and he placed his hand clumsily on her shoulder.

"It's…" she said, "it's like something had happened long ago. I never really expected him to come back, Benjamin."

Patiently, she would mourn, letting go slowly of the past, reminiscing of what had been, of wonderful years with him…loving years.

Her children would become her entire life now. Zane was again foreman of *The Crossing*, and he and Judith were soon to be married. And should Benjamin live, he would surely marry, and she would live her life through her grandchildren.

Grandchildren! How Judah would have longed to be a part of their lives…but now…..

Over the next several months, when possible, Dan weaved himself in and out of her life. When he was in Columbia, he would bring her little gifts. A handkerchief, a soft hairbrush, little gifts a woman would appreciate. She was on his mind constantly. In his foolishness he had nearly allowed himself to be taken by rebel guerrillas, so engrossed he was by thoughts of her.

The time came that he would ask for her hand in marriage. He arrived unexpectedly, as usual, on her doorstep one evening.

She invited him to share her supper, and when dinner was over they went into the parlor.

Dan appeared nervous, she thought. Had something happened to Benjamin?

"Is something on your mind, Dan? Is it Benjamin?"

He coughed, and then cleared his throat.

"No. Benjamin is fine. I've come, Marnie, to ask for your hand in marriage."

At her look of surprise, he continued with hands fanned wide, "I know it may be considered an inappropriate length of time since Judah died, but I've been waiting for years…waiting for you, Marnie. You must know how I feel about you. I've loved you for these past three years. If you feel you need more time to wait so that folks won't talk, I'm willing. But, please, just say yes."

She looked at him, heart in his eyes. She had a great depth of feeling for him. Feeling that had grown over these years. She missed him tremendously when he had stayed away for so long. Did she love him? Is that what you would call it? She thought she did…but in a different way from Judah, nevertheless, a love that was still there.

Marnie abruptly told him she would have to pray about it.

CHAPTER THIRTY-SIX

DAN FELT HIS HEART tearing within him. He liked to avoid good-byes, and this was leading to one. He fiddled with the girth, rearranged the saddlebags, trying to postpone this timeless moment.

He turned to her once again. Dan put his hand under her chin, quietly turned her face up. His eyes met hers, searching eyes, taking in every aspect of her face as his mouth opened with wordless words and then closed again. He had no doubt. He would never meet another woman like her again.

"I've been saying good-bye to you over and over again for hours," he said. "Seeing you does not make it any easier."

Marnie. Marnie Cross. Her name would always be etched in his mind in memory. The look of her face, the color of her eyes and hair, the easy way she had of walking, her laughter, and yes…her undefeatable spirit.

Seeing the struggle written plainly on her face, Dan dropped his hand and turned to leave. There was no indication, no hopeful smile that she would come into his arms and say yes.

Why was it, she thought, that she could not close the chapter on Judah and move on with her life with someone else? Was God asking her to devote her life to him and live in celibacy? There was a feeling so strong within her that would not allow her to marry Dan

Cable. What was this feeling? So often in the last few weeks she had labored in prayer about it all and was left without answers.

Mounting his horse, he looked at her one last time, lingering long, taking in every detail of her to store in memory. Something about what he felt then was to remain with him, never to leave him again. He then started away.

Her heart turned over within her. He was riding out of her life…this man who had been there for her, understood her, and protected her. He was leaving and taking part of her heart with him.

Dear, Lord, how can I let him go?

"Wait," she said urgently, taking a step towards him, and at that word he halted his horse.

"I just want to say—" and she paused, for that seemed the only appropriate thing to do.

There was silence—and the silence was expectant, filled with heartfelt things she could not say.

He waited for her to finish without looking back at her. When she didn't, he slowly started his horse again, hoping she would call out once more, expecting her to say yes.

Yet, she didn't. What could she say that had not already been said?

He was riding slowly away, out of her present, out of her future, out of her life.

Marnie watched, standing very still, framing every part of him in her mind as he rode down the drive. She watched as he turned onto the road until the woods swallowed him up and he was completely out of sight, and even then she did not move, but stood there, silent and alone in the middle of the yard, the staccato hoofbeats of Dan's horse growing fainter and fainter in the air until there was no more sound.

She knew she would never forget him, and never forget those perilous, yet wonderful times together.

She touched her lips with the backs of her fingers, lips that had never been kissed by him. Lips that wanted kissing, yet always…always something within her denied him that pleasure.

Tears welled in her eyes for she knew her time with him was over. Suddenly she wanted to cry, to lie down on the grass and sob endlessly. It had been exciting, but there were no more tomorrows to look forward to with him. She had lost two men. Judah was dead, and now, at the last, Dan Cable was gone from her, too. It was nearly too much for her to bear. How could she face the future? In desperation, she wanted to cry aloud, "What do you expect from me, God?"

She waited. It wasn't long.

I can do all things through Christ which strengtheneth me.

She quieted at that Scripture. The tension went out of her shoulders and they slumped, a quiet resignation, a quiet submission. She still had Judith, and for the present, Benjamin.

But then, stubbornly, a small ember tried to flare into a flame of emotion, and she thought, "But I can't let him go! Dear God, if you would just send him back to me."

Nevertheless not my will, but thine, be done.

There was finality in those words and the silence that ensued.

Marnie wiped her eyes with the back of her hand and sniffed.

She looked again at the place where Dan had disappeared, and she knew that he would not be back…not this time. Her heart yearned toward the way his horse had gone and remembered that somber, lonely expression of his eyes.

His memory would remain something to be cherished, something to be loved, something belonging to them only.

She knew when tomorrow came and all tomorrows after that, she would think of him, even as she did of Judah. She had heard that time eased the loss, had heard it told to numerous widows and children whose men had died in the war by well-meaning people wanting to assuage the pain. Until time wended its way through its unstoppable course, she would wait…wait for that moment when memory no longer caused sorrow, but rather became a cherished possession.

"Thank you," she finally whispered to where he had vanished, and hoped her words would be carried on the wind. She gave him all she had for that was all she could give, and she knew he wanted more than "Thanks".

CHAPTER THIRTY-SEVEN

MARNIE HAD JUST LEFT Tess Banyon's little house. Tess was to be married to Harry Kessler in two weeks time, and Marnie was helping her prepare her wedding dress. She would be sorry to see her leave *The Crossing*. It would not be the same without her as she had lived here over twenty years.

Heading toward home, Marnie stopped and sniffed the air and smiled. It was 1865 and spring would soon arrive, her favorite time of year. It was a time of new beginnings, new life, and planning for crops. The sun was shining, trees were budding, yellow jonquils were once again blooming. She bent and picked one, admiring its beauty. She felt like skipping as she did as a child, but knew anyone looking would think her silly. The mantle of widowhood was upon her, but she suddenly felt a lifting of sorrow.

Strange she should feel that way, and as she walked, tried to analyze what she was feeling. A soft wind began to blow and it was as though she heard voices in the breeze. Judah's voice. She gave her head a little shake at the voice she imagined she was hearing.

Reaching her front steps, she was preparing to climb when, upon hearing faint footfalls of someone coming up the gravel drive, she swung about, rigid as a pointer, staring at a solitary soldier, clad in a ragged uniform that, from its telling, had seen many a gruesome day. He was a bearded man, feet dragging slowly up the drive, leaning on a cane. An emaciated figure, he was, with hair past his shoulders. His eyes remained fixed on Marnie as he approached.

Something about this man looked familiar. There was a faint stirring in her mind as a vague recollection probed her memory. She watched as the soldier closed the distance between them, then: with the impact of a blow, Marnie knew the truth. She couldn't believe what she was seeing. Her eyes were wide with astonishment and her hand gripped the railing as though it were a lifeline to her.

Judah! But, how could this be? Judah died at Andersonville Prison, was the report she had received. But here he was, alive, advancing toward her, though so thin, so pitifully thin, yet alive! Everything about him was changed, altered, except for his eyes. She would know those eyes anywhere, and right now there was a noticeable tension in them.

Her hand slipped from the rail and her heart leaped as he stopped in front of her. She felt the old longing rekindle within her and she wanted to throw herself into his arms, but something in his gaze stopped her cold.

Trembling, frightened, a sudden feeling of loneliness upon her, she stared at him, becoming lost in his watchful eyes.

He stood, as though waiting for some word, some response from her…something she couldn't quite define. Would he rebuff her now for her parting words? Words spoken that were intended to wound him as she had felt by his leaving her?

She remembered his parting words to her. *Marnie, I need your prayers for the journey ahead of me.*

Yet, she had not promised her prayers, for resentment had risen up strong and hard within her and had stung her.

Was everything over between them now? The years of living together as man and wife, bearing two children, working side by side with him in his profession as a doctor?

Her throat was so tight it seemed she had swallowed shards of glass.

Without saying a word, and leaning on his cane, Judah looked down at her with a startling intensity. He hesitated, stood still as if waiting for her to settle the matter between them. For a long moment they just looked at one another, as if getting their bearings after years apart. Was he remembering her departure so long ago at *The Crossing*? Her angry words spoken to hurt him returned to her and reverberated in her mind, cutting her as it had him. Could the chasm she created between them now be crossed? Would he forgive her? Would he take her in his arms, or was it too late?

Marnie turned her head, unable to look at him…unable to bear both his pain and hers.

She began to step away, but his hand took her arm and stopped her. Without a word spoken, she was drawn to look at him again.

He saw the anxious look in her eyes...often-thought regrets for the past, and he knew. He always knew. She could never hide anything from him, and she had been, at times, furious and indignant at her own transparency. But now, suddenly she was glad. Glad that he knew her inside and out…still did, after all these years.

Her jaw trembled and her lips parted with unspoken words, and her heart, once again, was in her face.

Marnie stilled her trembling and in her uncertainty, her voice was shaky, a bit disbelieving.

"Judah."

His eyes suddenly glistened.

Could this be tears she was seeing or was she mistaken? To her amazement it was, for a tear found its way down his cheek, disappearing in his beard. Marnie was astonished beyond words for Judah never cried, never really revealed his entire heart. He had been closer, though, to her, than anyone else. They had been one in their marriage, his love more revealing to her than any other, yet there was always something he reserved for himself.

As her awe deepened of his raw emotion, her pride softly ebbed away and she lifted her hand to capture his tear. Her fingers lingered there, waiting, hoping for some acknowledgement from him that he had forgiven her.

Slowly, he lifted his hand, covered hers with his own, closed his eyes, and pressed her hand into his cheek.

"Marnie," he said simply, and for a time he was silent. She waited for more. When he finally spoke again, it was as though a wall within him had given way and he said softly: "My Marnie."

When those words left his lips, she felt an unburdening deep inside her, a softening and healing. Something had broken within her. It no longer mattered that he had left her behind...that he had gone to fight a war she didn't believe in. He was here...now...at *The Crossing* with her.

"Oh, Judah," she softly cried, "Can you ever forgive me?"

It seemed an eternity before he opened his eyes and answered. "No, I can't," he finally answered.

An arrow pierced her heart, and it was fatal. Her hand unconsciously slipped from his cheek, on its way to cover her aching heart.

"There's," he continued after several seconds, "nothing to forgive."

She'd forgotten the sound of his voice, but now hearing it again, she wept, the sob coming freely to Marnie's throat even as her head found its way onto his neck, her head tucked in the hollow place between his chest and shoulder. He wrapped his tired arm around her shoulder, drawing her closer.

She leaned into him, feeling his warmth, knowing suddenly this is the way it must be, not only now, but always.

"You're here. You're really here," she said, wonder filling her voice.

His mouth was warm against her ear. "I told you I'd come back."

After a time, she lifted her head, wiped her cheeks. "But, Judah," she said, a bit disbelieving, "they—they reported to me that you were dead."

There was the faintest trace of a smile on his face. “So they thought,” he answered. “The man next to me was scheduled to be transferred to Camp Lawton, at Savannah, Georgia, but he died in the night, and I traded places with him, took on his identity. It seems as though I’m still listed as deceased at Andersonville. Ironically, I was sent back to Andersonville before Sherman came through. Camp Lawton was destroyed by Sherman. From Andersonville, President Lincoln finally allowed exchanges once again.”

Judah smiled a haunting smile. “The war is nearly over, Marnie,” he told her. “We can pick up our lives where we left off and begin again.”

There was a meeting of the minds between them, when the world and time stand aside, and there was only the here and now.

He leaned in and kissed her, then…a slow, long, leisurely kiss. A kiss that dismissed any reserve he’d held in the past, a kiss that gave his heart fully to her.

“You never kissed me like that before,” she told him when they pulled apart.

“I…always meant to,” he confessed.

Suddenly, Marnie was young again as the troubles of the war took flight from her mind and they lost their power to wound her. The past was in the past. With the rousing of fresh hope, her regrets now had no standing. The war was not over yet, however, her struggles of the last few years would soon become just a memory.

Before her stretched many tomorrows of hope, healing, and dreaming of dreams, for—

Judah had come home.

About the Author

A graduate of Chatfield College and from a family of several ministers, Donna Whitaker has pastored several churches, and served as evangelist, missionary, songwriter, recording artist, musician, and teacher. Speaking at various venues, she has also served as spokeswoman and praise and worship leader with Aglow International, the women's division of The Full Gospel Businessmen's Association.

Donna's own family has a history in the areas her novels are set in. Of Scottish descent and the well-known Sinclair family, Donna can trace her ancestor sailing on the ship *Loyalty* to North America in 1698 and follow her family's progress from Virginia to Adair County, Kentucky in the very early 1800's. Church and courthouse records document Alexander Sinclair, her 4th great grandfather, as an ordained minister of that county.

On her maternal side, Donna is descended from Brigadier General Jesse Richardson, a Revolutionary War soldier who also served under General George Rogers Clark. One of the first settlers of Pulaski County, Kentucky, General Richardson was elected to the Kentucky State Legislature as the first senator of Pulaski and Cumberland Counties in 1800.

Interacting with people from many walks of life has given Donna an understanding of people and helped to make her an effective story teller.

Donna resides in southern Ohio.

Donna may be contacted at donnajeanwhitaker@gmail.com

www.ingramcontent.com/pod-product-compliance
Lightning Source LLC
LaVergne TN
LVHW090602110826
845146LV00001B/233

* 9 7 9 8 2 3 4 0 4 7 1 2 0 *